SW

THE TOFF AND THE GOLDEN BOY

An outbreak of robberies with threatened violence on small tobacconist shops in London, involving gangs of long-haired youths led by Golden Boy, has the Toff searching for a motive, especially as the profits are so small. What is it that gives Golden Boy such a hold over these boys? When several attempts are made on the Toff's life in an effort to make him drop the case, it becomes apparent that much more is involved than profits from small shop raids. Whatever the risks, he has to find out.

THE TOFF
AND THE
GOLDEN BOY

John Creasey

First published 1969
by
Hodder & Stoughton Ltd
This edition 1993 by Chivers Press
published by arrangement with
the author's estate

ISBN 0 7451 8607 6

British Library Cataloguing in Publication Data available

Printed and bound in Great Britain by
Redwood Press Limited, Melksham, Wiltshire

FOREWORD

It is always a privilege to be invited to contribute an introduction to a work by a popular favourite, but I was especially grateful to be given this opportunity with a John Creasey title.

It was in January 1960 when I attended my first meeting of the Crime Writers' Association. In those days the meetings were held at Whitehall Court, opposite what was then Scotland Yard. As a new member, and with only two books to my credit at the time, I entered the room with some trepidation. A smiling man came up to me, hand outstretched, and said 'Hallo, you must be new. I'm John Creasey. Come and meet some of the others.' A totally charming, unaffected man, he introduced me to a host of celebrities, all of whom made me welcome. I was unaware then that John was the founder of the CWA and the driving force behind it. He it was who set the pattern for the informal bonhomie of the Association and, as with so many aspects of his life, he led from the front.

Any author will tell you, with a wry smile, of the people one meets who confide that they keep meaning to write a book but can never find the time. I sometimes wonder what they would have made of John Creasey. He contrived to find time to write not just one book, but almost six hundred of them, the majority with themes of crime and/or detection. The walls of the library/study of his lovely home outside Salisbury were lined with this vast collection, together with translations. A stringent reference system was essential in order to keep track of it all. At the last assessment a couple of years ago worldwide sales amounted to over sixty million copies, a figure which continues to rise, and deservedly so.

John Creasey used more than twenty pseudonyms in the course of this mammoth output, creating several series characters in the process. One of the most successful of these was the Honourable Richard Rollison, the Toff, a wealthy, upper-crust character with a penchant for involving himself in dubious, frequently dangerous situations, preferably with a dewy-eyed maiden or two in the offing. He made his first appearance in the early 1930s and came complete, as did many of his contemporary gentleman-adventurers, with a trusty manservant, Jolly, and a Mayfair address. He was equally at home in the Royal enclosure and the lowest of dockside taverns. So popular were these stories that Creasey featured him in no less than fifty-eight full-length novels.

The title you are about to enjoy is a prime example of the series.

A gang of youths carry out a series of robberies on small shopkeepers, tobacconists and sweetshops in London's East End. The raids take place with great audacity in broad daylight, with skill and obvious organisation which is quite disproportionate to the value of the haul. The leader is a good-looking, well-dressed youth with golden hair, who terrorises the victims into silence with threats of violent reprisals if they give the police any useful descriptions.

The Toff is a regular visitor at the Blue Dog public house in White-chapel, where he keeps in touch with developments in London's underworld. The landlord, Bill Ebbutt, is so incensed about the mounting reign of terror that he takes the unusual step of calling on the Honourable Richard at his West End flat. 'Mr Ar', as Bill calls him, quickly contacts an old friend and sometimes adversary in the person of the formidable Superintendent Bill Grice.

It transpires that the operations of the gang have already extended beyond the limits of the East End, and are becoming widespread. Police investigation is seriously hampered by the lack of cooperation from the victims, who are all thoroughly cowed by the threats from Golden Boy and his cohorts. The notable exception is Jack Slater, one of the younger shopkeepers, who has armed himself with a Luger, and is muttering about reprisals of his own, which is not at all the public response the police are seeking.

The Toff is intrigued by the scale of the gang's activities, and becomes convinced there is some wider motive for these well-organised attacks than the obvious one of the trifling direct profits. His intervention quickly becomes known to Golden Boy, who warns him that he will be killed if he persists. Unlike many criminals, the youth is not uttering empty threats, and an attempt on the Toff's life quickly follows.

To reveal any more would be to spoil your pleasure, quite the opposite of my intent. I hope I have said enough to whet your appetite and, as they used to say in the days of the instalment magazines, 'Now read on . . .'

PETER CHAMBERS

Peter Chambers is a former Chairman of the CWA, and the author of over sixty crime and detective books, some featuring his own 'private eye' in an imaginary California town, and others under various *noms de plume*.

THE BLACK DAGGER CRIME SERIES

The Black Dagger Crime series is a result of a joint effort between Chivers Press and a sub-committee of the Crime Writers' Association, consisting of Marian Babson, Peter Chambers and Peter Lovesey. It is designed to select outstanding examples of every type of detective story, so that enthusiasts will have the opportunity to read once more classics that have been scarce for years, while at the same time introducing them to a new generation who have not previously had the chance to enjoy them.

CONTENTS

CHAPTER ONE

THE OLD COUPLE

'WE'LL be all right, dear,' old Penryn said. 'There's nothing worth taking from this little shop. There's no need to worry.'

'It's all very well to *say* there isn't,' Martha Penryn retorted. 'But I don't like the way they stand at the window and stare. It's almost as if they were sizing the place up.'

'You worry too much,' said Joshua.

Yet afterwards, when he was alone in the tobacconist's and confectioner's shop which he and Martha had built up from nothing, he was uneasy. It *was* small, with a variety of popular brands of cigarettes and tobacco as well as cigars on one side, chocolates and sweets in glass jars on the other. It was colourful and had a clean smell, and was, in fact, spotless. Opposite the front door, leading to Merrihew Street, near the Whitechapel Road, was the door into the back room where small stocks were kept. For the most part the local wholesalers serviced all their supplies, and they had no need to store them in quantity. The back room, therefore, was also a sitting room, and beyond it was a small kitchen. Upstairs were two bedrooms and a bathroom.

This was the Penryns' home; and life.

Martha was upstairs, resting; at sixty-nine, a woman needed to rest after lunch. Joshua, still troubled by his wife's apprehension, lifted the flap in the counter and strolled to the street door. Few people were about, their trade came in predictable rushes—before work, at lunch time, and after work. Within a few hundred yards were several warehouses and two small factories—the employees working at them, and neighbours in the small houses nearby, comprised the shop's regular customers.

Joshua stepped on to the pavement—and his heart missed a beat, for approaching from the warehouse end of the street were four youths.

He was tempted to turn back into the shop, but if he did they might think he was frightened. So he pretended to look beyond them, to Morgan's place, where a variety of small, cheap toys were made.

This part of London's East End had changed very little in fifty years.

Beyond Morgan's two-storey factory new apartment buildings rose, like boxes with pieces bitten out of the corners. Washing hung dejectedly from some of the balconies. It was a muggy day, a film of moisture covering pavements and roadway, the roofs of a dozen parked cars, the shop fronts, the window boxes where the bright colours of phlox and asters were dimmed by the grey mist which might soon turn to rain.

The four youths drew closer, talking quietly among themselves. There was insolence in their manner, a kind of arrogance which, in the spirit of the times, seemed to fall like a cloak over so many young people. Three were long-haired, wore old tunics and narrow trousers, and looked as if they could do with a bath; all of these had dark, stubble-shadowed cheeks and chins.

The fourth, much shorter, had beautiful, golden-coloured hair. He had clear blue eyes and looked too young to shave. He was dressed in an orthodox pale grey suit, and wore a blue bow tie.

Joshua Penryn looked the other way.

There was the Whitechapel Road, busy with traffic, big red buses lumbering past, cars and taxis and huge great trucks going to and from the docks. Yet these sounds of London's thriving trade were muted, for Merrihew Street was very long, and they seemed so far away.

The footsteps of the four youths drew nearer.

If only he had stayed in the shop, thought Joshua—he need not have appeared to notice them. Now he would have to step back out of their path and into the doorway of his shop—or else make *them* go round him.

He felt a sudden flare of resentment which made him almost forget his fear. Once upon a time, he thought, once upon a time he would have sent these young louts about their business, they wouldn't have come four abreast, obviously determined to make him stand aside.

Then he caught sight of Martha in the shop. The flare of passion died, too agitated to rest, her fear communicated itself to him. He stepped into the doorway.

'. . . dy old fool,' one of the long-haired louts said.

'Good thing he got out of our way.'

'Who does he think he is?'

'Ought to put them away when they get *that* old,' said the boy with the golden-coloured hair, in a voice that was honey-sweet.

Joshua flushed, right round the nape of his neck, and clenched his hands—but pretended not to notice. Martha was only just on the other side of the door, looking so old and frail.

'Good thing he knows his place,' one lout said.

'We'd have taught him.'

'Silly old basket.'

'You've got to admit it,' said the golden-haired boy, 'the Nazis had something when they got rid of the old.'

His voice was as clear and as close as it had been when he had first spoken, which meant that they hadn't moved on.

Martha was beckoning and calling to him—he could see her lips moving but could not hear a word.

Then a blessed thing happened—Toby's van appeared from the factory end of the street. Toby's were the wholesalers who supplied their sweets and chocolates, and Bert Something-or-other was a big hefty man in the early forties who would stand no nonsense. The youths, muttering words which Joshua could not catch, walked on.

Martha snatched the door open.

'That's them!' she gasped. 'They're the ones who were staring in this morning.'

'Now stop worrying, Martha,' said Joshua, sounding much bolder than he felt. 'Have you done the list for Toby's?'

'Of course I have.'

'He's just coming,' Joshua said, and a moment later the van drew up and Bert jumped down and came in, whistling.

'Hallo, Pop—hi, Ma!' He had a deep, booming voice. 'Anything for me today?' He was so bright and breezy and natural that he drove Joshua's fears away. He went out to get their goods from the van and Martha said:

'You ought to tell him.'

'What ought I to tell him?'

'About that *gang*.'

'There's nothing to tell him,' Joshua protested. 'We're not going to make him think we're scared, are we?'

'If you're not, *I* am,' said Martha forthrightly, and as the door opened again she went on almost in the same breath: 'Bert, do you know anything about those louts who just passed?'

'Louts? What louts?'

'Didn't you see them?' Martha demanded, almost angrily.

'Bert was coming round the corner,' Joshua said placatingly.

'Have to keep me eye on the road,' Bert said bluffly. He put a box of bars of chocolate and two bottles on the counter, took out an invoice pad, and made out a list, with a carbon copy. Finished, he said: 'Four pounds one and fourpence, Mr. Penryn—I've taken the usual two and a half off for cash.'

Joshua went behind the counter and pressed a till tab; the till drawer sprang open. Carefully he counted out the money, as carefully Bert scrawled 'paid' across the invoice and added his signature.

With a grin, and a casual wave of his hand, he went off whistling.

'I'm *sure* they were the ones who were watching,' Martha said. 'I can't understand how Bert missed them.'

'Now stop worrying and go back to bed!' said Joshua sharply.

'Oh, I shan't *sleep*. I happened to look out of the window, and I saw them. Did they speak to you?'

'No,' said Joshua, as the van drove off.

Almost immediately afterwards a young woman with a child in a pram, another at her knee, and a third on the way, came in for some peppermints and an ice lolly. Martha waved goodbye to the older child as they left the shop.

And as they disappeared, the golden-haired boy loomed suddenly in the doorway. One youth was close behind him, two others stood on either side of the door, in a position to watch the whole street.

The boy said: 'Don't want to get hurt, do you?'

'What—what do you mean?' demanded Joshua, his voice shrill.

'What I say. Just stand perfectly still. And don't move.' His voice was still honeyed. He looked scarcely more than a child. 'And if you keep your mouths shut you won't get hurt.'

The other youth sprang over the counter and began to load packets of cigarettes and tobacco into a sack. The golden-haired boy flicked open another and began to pack the chocolate into it. They worked very swiftly, making little sound.

'That—that's thieving!' gasped Martha.

'You don't say——'

'You've no right——' Joshua began.

'Shut your mouth,' the boy said, 'if you don't want a bottle broken over your head.' He went on taking the chocolates. 'Now listen. If you squawk you'll get hurt. Okay, so you can say you were robbed, but if you give a description of us we'll soon find out and *you'll* know all about it. That goes for you too, Ma,' he went on. 'Remember Ma Fitch?'

Martha made a frightened sound.

'That's right, she talked too much—and hey presto! Someone wrung her neck,' the boy said, and in the same dulcet tones, he went on: 'Okay, Fred?'

'Okay.'

'Okay outside?'

The two youths glanced round and cocked their thumbs.

'Just forget what we look like,' the boy said.

He stood with his back to the street, raised his hand slowly from his pocket, and showed a closed knife. He touched it and a sharp, glistening blade shot out. He made a slashing gesture with the knife and bared his teeth.

In that instant he looked both ugly and vicious.

'Don't talk,' he said, and went out.

The door slammed.

The old couple stood, as if petrified, staring as a fifth youth came up at the wheel of a small station wagon. The sacks were tossed in, all four got in the car, and the little vehicle moved off.

Slowly, agonisingly, Joshua stared at the empty shelves; at the odd packets which had been dropped to the floor and trampled. To the open till. He felt as if a great weight were pressing on his head, and in those few minutes he was oblivious of Martha.

She made a little sobbing sound. He turned to see her—and to see the tears welling up in her eyes. He put an arm about her, in empty comfort, feeling the trembling of her body. Soon she was wracked with crying, for so much had gone, so much they had striven for—*slaved* for.

A small boy came into the shop, saw them, glanced towards the almost empty chocolate counter, and, after what must have seemed an age to him, said:

'Can I have a sixpenny lolly, please?'

'Six—sixpenny lolly,' gasped Martha. 'And we've lost nearly all our worldly possessions!'

The boy turned and ran out, scared. He ran to his mother, and she came to find out what was wrong; it was she who telephoned the police, and within a few minutes a police car pulled up outside, two of its doors opened at once, and two youngish men descended without haste. They began to ask questions—question after question, which seemed to go on and on.

Somebody always knew somebody who knew the Toff.

Some knew him only by that light-hearted but well-deserved soubriquet, for he was generous and understanding with the less fortunate. A few considered that the generosity and understanding reached dangerously near to the point of tolerating the breaking of the law. Others knew him—even those in the rough, tough East End of London—by his full name, the Honourable Richard Rollison. And most of his friends called him Rolly.

At times there seemed to be a hot line between his expensive Mayfair flat and his unofficial headquarters in the East End—the Blue Dog. The Blue Dog was a pub in a street in White-chapel, and it was owned by one William (Bill) Ebbutt, who also owned a gymnasium-cum-boxing academy close by. Everybody who was anybody frequented either the pub or the gym; including Joshua Penryn and his Martha—regular Satur-day nighters in the saloon bar—and Bert Williams, who drove for Toby's—regular every nighter.

On the morning after the raid on the little shop in Merrihew Street, first one and then another asked Bill Ebbutt whether he'd heard; and wasn't it disgraceful; and who the hell was behind it? And how many raids was this, now? And why *couldn't* the police take action? And if they couldn't, who could?

Ebbutt, a huge, wheezing asthmatic who had trained more champions than any man in London, left the Blue Dog and plodded to the shop, which was closed, and banged on the door until old Joshua came to see who it was—and was shocked to see how this lively, likeable man had aged in a matter of hours.

Ebbutt asked as many questions as the police.

An hour later, exasperated, he left Joshua and Martha and

went back to the Blue Dog, saying to the crony who had been in charge during his absence:

'Well, that's that, then. If the Toff (he pronounced it Torf) won't come and find out about it, *I'm* going to the West End to tell him. Go and get me car out.'

CHAPTER TWO

THE TOFF

IT was a warm day in late June. The windows were open in the big living-room at Rollison's flat in Gresham Terrace, so the noise of the ancient engine sounded clearly in the ears of Rollison himself, his Aunt Georgina, her twin children George and Geraldine who were young enough to call Rollison, their cousin, uncle, and a very attractive young woman who was no relation—and Jolly.

Jolly was the Honourable Rollison's man.

It is true, no doubt, that Rollison himself was an anachronism, a hangover from the days of knights in shining armour, but Jolly, in his way, was no less so. He still, for instance, wore winged collars and grey cravats, and addressed his employer with a certain punctilious deference. Still, he was human enough to expand at the attractive young woman's request for an explanation of 'the wall'.

She was referring to the Trophy Wall, and everything that was on it, no matter how sinister or macabre.

Those who knew Rollison well found it hard to believe there had been a time when no Trophy Wall existed, and the older exhibits now on it had been kept in a kind of bottom drawer. But it was so. Jolly had held the key of this drawer, and it had been a long, wordless struggle for Rollison to get the trophies out of the drawer and on to the wall. With that remarkable facility—common to some women, and a few faithful servants —for changing his mind with such entirety that any reference to his former opinion was met with pained disbelief, Jolly had become converted. With his own hands, saw, and electric drill, he had established the wall as it was now.

It was quite remarkable.

On small shelves, in little glass cases, in recesses, on hooks and hangers, was a miscellany of weapons, each of which had been lawlessly used to kill.

This, Jolly gravely expounded to the Toff's latest admirer.

'All *these*,' she breathed in disbelief.

'Fifty, miss,' said Jolly, proudly.

'And—and Mr. Rollison caught them *all*?'

'Let us say that without his help they would certainly not have been caught,' amended Jolly, tactfully.

'But *fifty*!' The young woman—whose name was Miranda —touched a diaphanous-looking piece of nylon draped over a carved wooden leg which had no foot beyond the ankle. 'Did *that* kill someone?'

'Three young women were strangled with that stocking, miss.'

Miranda looked as if the information gave her a delicious thrill.

'And those chicken feathers?'

'That is a rather longer story, miss. If you would care to hear . . .' Jolly paused, and glanced towards the window where the two cousins stood, and through which the improbable sound came. One of them glanced out, and said: 'Good God!'

'George, how often must I tell you not to use "God" as an expletive?' demanded his mother, who was fifty-seven years old and steeped in the respect and reverence of the generation which had given her birth.

She was, in fact, unfortunate in many ways, for her husband had been what her family called a 'bounder'. A Member of Parliament with a minor ministerial post, he had used this position of privilege to spend other people's money. Unwise enough to be found out he had appealed to Rollison in an endeavour to avoid the threatened scandal.

Rollison, weary of financial help that had simply egged him on to further depredations, refused. It was, no doubt, partly due to this refusal that his Aunt Georgina's husband had killed himself.

Rollison did not like Georgina, nor did he have any special regard for her children; but because of a lurking sense of guilt he had always given them more time and consideration than other relations. Probably only Jolly knew of this.

Now, Jolly was glancing at the window from where George called:

'But ye Gods, look!'

His twin sister, sweet Geraldine, pressed closer.

Rollison, standing over six feet, still dark-haired and by all standards handsome, did not need to look out of the window, and yet he did so. Approaching this house, 22 Gresham Terrace, was yet another anachronism—a Model T Ford. It was polished and burnished and painted bright blue. A dozen people in the street turned and stared towards it. Sitting at the wheel was enormous Bill Ebbutt, who had twice driven his car in the Brighton old crocks' race. It drew up outside the house, while all watched with bated breath as Ebbutt majestically descended.

'. . . never seen anything like it,' breathed George.

'He's coming *here*!' gasped Geraldine.

'He's an old friend of mine,' stated Rollison.

'*Friend?*' echoed George and Geraldine.

'Good friend,' Rollison said, and glanced at Jolly.

'If you will excuse me, miss,' Jolly was saying to Miranda. He saw the way Rollison's gaze swivelled towards the door, and immediately went towards it.

'. . . and I must say you have some remarkable friends,' said Aunt Georgina. 'It really *is* time we were going.'

'Oh, no!' groaned George, her son.

'Must we?' pleaded Geraldine. 'He looks gorgeous!'

'I've only heard a *half* of what I'd like to hear,' said George.

'Don't let Bill Ebbutt drive you away,' said Rollison without enthusiasm. 'Jolly will make sure whether he wants to talk to me in confidence or not.'

As he spoke, there was a ring at the front door bell.

Soon, Ebbutt appeared and Jolly announced:

'Mr. William Ebbutt, sir.'

Mine host of the Blue Dog sported, for this occasion, a dark suit with a purple weave, a green tie stabbed with a pin bearing a boxing glove, and brown shoes. He had a big head, pendulous jowls, no neck to speak of, and a huge chest merging into a mammoth waist-line. All the time he breathed, he wheezed. The brightness of his periwinkle blue eyes, almost buried in flesh, was remarkable.

Rollison introduced him.

'Sorry to butt in, Mr. Ar,' he said when he was settled with a glass of beer in his hand, 'but I'm a bit worried by something that's going on down our way.' He knew of course that he was free to talk, or he would not have been brought in here, and he went on: 'There's been a lot of nasty little raids on small shops——'

'A lot?' interrupted Rollison.

'Well, far more than can be expected in the normal run of petty crime.'

'Over how long a period?'

'Couple of months, or more,' answered Ebbutt, and when Rollison kept silent, he went on: 'There's a gang of young louts—about this young gentleman's age, begging your pardon, sir—who raid shops with stock that's easy to sell; packet goods, sweets and chocolate, cigarettes and tobacco, that kind of thing. They scare the wits out of the shopkeepers and get away with it.'

He paused, and Rollison said: 'Police.'

'There's one thing they all seem to have in common,' said Ebbutt, a frown corrugated his forehead into rows of deep furrows and nearly buried his eyes. 'None of the victims will *talk*. Won't describe the young brutes—they say they didn't see them properly, or the thieves wore stockings over their faces. So the police can't get very far.'

'I suppose not,' said Rollison dubiously. 'What made you come today?'

'To tell you the truth, it was a raid yesterday on a shop in

Merrihew Street, round the corner from me—you know. Josh and Martha Penryn—been there for years. I went round to see them, and Josh told *me* something he never told the cops, Mr. Ar. I thought it time I come and had a talk with you—ought to have come before, I suppose.'

'What did he tell you?' asked Rollison.

George and Geraldine, Miranda, and Lady Georgina were staring first at Ebbutt and then at Rollison in a mixture of incredulity and wonder. A beading of sweat greyed Ebbutt's brow and he took out a folded white handkerchief with purple edges and mopped both his brow and his upper lip.

'They told me what scared them,' he answered.

'What did?'

'They said that if they talked they'd get the same as old Ma Fitch.'

To the guests, this statement meant nothing. To Jolly and Rollison it conveyed a great deal, reminding them, as it did, of the elderly woman who had lived most of her life in a corner shop, and had been savagely strangled. The murder had sent a shudder through the whole of the East End, and the hue and cry had been quite outstanding.

That had been twelve months ago—and the murderers, two youths, had been caught and were now serving life sentences in prison.

Miranda and the three G's had gone.

Ebbutt had gone.

Rollison and Jolly were together in the living-room, Rollison at a big desk with his back to the Trophy Wall, Jolly standing by it. Rollison had the telephone at his ear and the *burr-burr* of the ringing sound could clearly be heard.

'It would happen on Sunday,' Rollison said testily.

'Mr. Grice might have gone off for the week-end, sir.'

'The Yard said he was at home.'

Burr-burr, rang the bell in Grice's home; burr-burr—*eck*! A man said: 'Grice speaking.'

'Superintendent Grice?' asked Rollison, in his sweetest voice. '*The* Superintendent Grice?'

'Who is that?' demanded Grice, and then his tone changed: 'Oh, it's you, you ass. I hope it's something worth bringing me out of the garden for.'

'I think so, Bill,' said Rollison. 'But it's shop.'

'Urgent?'

'Not a matter of life and death,' Rollison admitted.

'Then give me a couple of hours, I'm stuck in the middle of cutting back some ramblers I ought to have done last year ... How about looking in for tea?'

'Good idea,' said Rollison. 'Four o'clock?'

'I'll be ready,' Grice promised.

Almost at that identical moment a young couple named Slater opened the door of a shop in Chelsea.

It was very like the Penryns' shop but of better quality and with a wider variety of goods for sale, including canned foods, paper-back books, and greetings cards. The shop had been closed for lunch, and now the Slaters opened it for their first Sunday afternoon's trading.

The couple from whom they had taken it over had assured them that there would be a steady flow of custom, even though the shop was not on a main street. The river was nearby, two cinemas, several big blocks of flats; and no other shop for some distance was open on Sunday. Jack Slater was in his late twenties. He had been a miner in the Midlands, and though he looked burly and strong, he had, in fact, been injured in a rock-fall three years earlier, and would never again have full power in his left arm. Jill, his wife, on the other hand, looked deceptively fragile. Long, limp hair falling untidily over really beautiful honey-brown eyes added to the look of fragility. Slender and willowy in build, she stood half-a-head taller than Jack, her husband of five years.

Jack behind the cigarette counter, Jill behind the sweets, they grinned at each other across the shop.

'Now let 'em all come,' Jack said.

'If we don't take twenty-five pounds this afternoon, we've been cheated,' Jill said, and, tossing back her hair, she added: 'Would it be a good idea if one of us went to the night-safe at the bank and put yesterday's takings in?'

'If we get slack,' said Jack Slater. 'Hallo—here's our first customer!'

A youth came in.

He looked very young. He had golden-coloured hair and a beautiful complexion, and when he spoke it was in honeyed tones. While he was speaking two other youths appeared, one from each direction. Jack noticed this but did not give it a thought beyond the fact that it seemed to prove how busy they were going to be on Sunday afternoons.

'Can I help you?' Jill said to one of them.

The golden-haired boy said: 'No thanks. We'll help ourselves.'

He drew his hand out of his pocket, with a single swift movement, and the blade sprang out with a sharp click. At the same time the others jumped over the counters, one on either side. They shook out sacks from beneath their coats and began to fill them, swiftly and expertly.

Jack roared: '*What the hell do you think you're doing?*'

'Robbing your shop,' said the boy with the golden hair.

Jack struck out at him, and at that moment the youth behind the counter pulled a cosh out of his waist-belt and smashed it down on Jack Slater's head. Jill rushed towards the back of the shop as her husband collapsed. The boy with the knife sprang after her, snatching at her hair, entwining his fingers in it and pulling savagely. Jill gasped with pain. The boy pulled again and said roughly:

'If you make any more fuss you'll really get hurt!'

'But my husband——'

'He'll live,' sneered the boy. He let her go but stayed watchful. There were scuffling noises as the stock was swept off the shelves into the sacks. A small car pulled up outside, the driver jumped out and beckoned. The golden-haired boy took something from his pocket—a plastic pepper pot. He flung the contents in Jill's face.

As she stood there, blinded and in pain, the raiders rushed to the car. It started off as half-a-dozen people turned the corner and headed for the shop.

CHAPTER THREE

GRICE'S GARDEN

AT two minutes past four Rollison turned into a street in Battersea, near the Bridge and the pleasure gardens, where Superintendent Grice had lived for several years. Most of the nearby houses were big and old-fashioned, but Grice's was one of half-a-dozen built on a site of an old house, long since demolished; and each owner was house and garden proud.

No one was more proud than Grice of the fact that at the far end of his garden were some old, rose-covered arches which had been there for twenty years. At the back of the house was a patch of bright green lawn, two narrow beds of flowers where his wife now worked, and—beyond them—a small vegetable garden. As Rollison's car drew up at the gate, Grice went to meet him, secateurs in hand.

'I'll put the kettle on in a few minutes,' said his wife. 'Don't let him come here and see me like this!' A tall, solidly-built woman with a good figure, she brushed greying hair out of her eyes as she spoke.

'If you're good enough for me,' said Grice, 'you're too good for the Toff!'

'Don't be ridiculous,' his wife said.

Rollison, hearing and seeing nothing of this, looked appreciatively at the mellowed-looking brick of the neo-Georgian house. Grice's pride in the garden was so obvious that he was mildly surprised to be taken straight into the house.

'You haven't been here before, have you?' Grice asked.

Rollison glanced admiringly round the tastefully furnished room. 'No. It's charming.'

'Ten minutes' walk from the river, ten from Battersea Park, half an hour by bus to almost anywhere in the heart of

London,' Grice said. 'I'm going to retire here.'

Rollison looked startled.

'Don't talk of retiring yet!'

'I'm ten years older than you,' said Grice. 'I finish in two years.'

Now Rollison looked quite shocked.

'I can't believe it,' he said, and studied the fine-drawn, sallow-complexioned face, the keen brown eyes, the high bridged nose over which the skin was stretched so taut it was almost white. There was a scar on Grice's face, from a wound received working on a case in which the Toff had been involved. 'Damn it, you're part of the Yard!'

'Unlike you and I, the Yard will go on for ever.'

'But you've so much specialised knowledge, it will be criminal to lose it.'

'There're plenty of youngsters coming along with the same knowledge, and a lot more technical know-how,' said Grice. 'I don't really belong to the age of transistors and computers. But let's sit down. Marion will bring some tea soon—she's quite excited at the thought of meeting you again.'

'I can't understand it,' said Rollison drily.

Grice smiled. 'What's brought you, Rolly?' That was like him—the sudden change of subject, the bringing together of all his faculties for concentration in a curiously piercing way.

Rollison said: 'I thought I'd consult you in advance for once. I——'

The telephone rang.

'Sorry,' said Grice. 'I'd better see what it is.' He moved, tall and lean, out of the room and picked up the telephone, his voice carrying easily. 'Grice speaking.' There was a short pause, and then: 'Just across the river ... Any descriptions? Humph ... Is he badly hurt? Something, then. What about his wife? I shouldn't wonder! Has Jackson been along? Well, have him call me as soon as he's made sure if it's the same gang...'

He rang off, leaving the word 'gang' floating in the air, an improbable word for this quiet house in this quiet street. When he came back he was frowning. He dropped into a chair and stretched out his legs, then spoke abruptly.

'You were about to say——'

Rollison chuckled.

'Nice to have you back! I was about to say that before I do anything about this particular job, I've come to see if you know much about it, and whether I'd just be wasting my time.'

'*You're* evidently approaching retiring age, too,' Grice observed.

Over their laugh, Rollison said: 'Bill Ebbutt came to see me this morning, worried about an old couple who were robbed yesterday—whose shop was robbed, rather. It seems to have been one in a long chain of incidents.'

'The latest of which, we think, was reported to me just now,' said Grice.

'Good God!' exclaimed Rollison, with no aunt to rebuke him. 'Across the river, you said. In Chelsea?'

'Yes.'

'But I thought they were all in the East End.'

'Which only goes to show that Ebbutt doesn't know everything,' Grice observed, with obvious satisfaction. 'Must have been at least five outside—spreading from Southwark to Camberwell. There was one in Fulham and now this affair in Chelsea. Chief Inspector Jackson's in charge—he won't like being dragged out on a Sunday afternoon, but he'll be able to tell us whether it's one of the series. Do you know Jackson?'

'Robert? The one who's nearly as broad as he's long?'

'That's the chap.'

'We met on a case, a year ago. Fairly tolerant, I remember, of me and my amateur meddling.'

'Jackson's a single-idea man—his aim is to get results, never mind how. Within reason,' added Grice hurriedly.

'And has he got them?'

'It's early days,' said Grice, a little uncomfortably. 'I wonder what he would say if you——' he broke off. 'I'll think about it.' He listened to footsteps on the stairs. 'That's Marion,' he remarked unnecessarily. 'Tea won't be long. Are you in any hurry?'

'No.'

'The significant features,' said Grice, with hardly a pause, 'are that the raids are carried out in broad daylight and to a kind of pattern. *Four* youths are usually involved in the raid itself, while one man drives a car. We suspect that the car is a different one every time—first stolen, and then abandoned after the job is done. Sacks are used to take the stolen goods away—we found some at one shop where the shopkeeper put up a fight—they're part of a big consignment stolen from a laundry firm a year ago. But that isn't all.'

'Well, what more is there?' asked Rollison.

'The Golden Boy.'

'The—*Golden* Boy?'

'A youth who looks about sixteen, has long and beautifully groomed golden hair, and the face of an angel,' Grice told him. 'He doesn't make the slightest attempt to disguise himself, though witnesses are extremely reluctant to describe him. We've taken thirty or forty of much the same type in for questioning and they've always been able to account for their movements. He appears to be the leader, and is certainly responsible for much of the violence. Where is he? What happens to him?'

'Can he be wearing a wig,' suggested Rollison.

'We thought of that,' retorted Grice. 'But in a tussle at one shop the shopkeeper pulled some of the hair out by the roots. It was under a microscope inside an hour—real hair, real roots, and the witness said the victim gave a real scream.'

Rollison mused: 'Puzzling is the word.'

Then Marion Grice came in, tidied, freshly made up. Her husband's eyes twinkled. After a few moments she went out and wheeled in a trolley bearing wafer-thin bread and butter, part of a rich fruit cake, and chocolate biscuits. Grice helped to arrange a tea tray laden with the best china and what looked like an early Georgian teapot and water jug. As he handed round the cups, they chatted about everything except crime, including the prospect of retirement. Then the telephone rang again.

'If it's one of the series, would you like to come?' asked Grice.

'Very much.'

Grice nodded, went out, and this time closed the door. His wife took Rollison's cup, emptied the dregs, began to pour out more, and asked:

'Is this another shop robbery?'

'Yes.'

'It's worrying him more than any case I can remember,' said Marion. 'It isn't the amount of money and goods stolen. That, as crime goes, is fairly negligible. It's the fact that the victims often aren't insured, they simply can't afford it. It's like robbing a church offertory box.' She handed over the cup, and went on: 'And it's the—the *insolence* of it. These youths just laugh at the police, and Bill's afraid that if it goes on much longer other raids might follow, by those who've nothing to do with the gang.'

She broke off, and for the second time that afternoon the word 'gang' hovered about the room.

Almost at once the door opened.

'The same lot all right,' said Grice. 'Off in ten minutes, Rolly. Sorry, dear—but I'll try not to be too late.'

It wasn't until they were driving off in Rollison's car that Grice said almost casually:

'Jackson will be glad of any help you can give him.'

'Police blessing at last,' murmured Rollison.

They turned out of the street towards Battersea Bridge, and Rollison saw the lovely grounds of the park, the sweep of the broad river as it curved towards Chelsea Bridge and Lambeth. At least a dozen pleasure boats, crammed with people, were in sight, and as many private craft, as well as moored barges.

London's skyline—the towering top of the Post Office, the great square blocks of offices and hotels—added a slightly futuristic, slightly alien air.

'I can understand why you want to retire here,' Rollison said.

'Always loved driving over this bridge,' said Grice, in a rare moment of self-disclosure. At the Yard, so very much the official, so concentrating on the immediate task, he was regarded, like Jackson, as being a man with a one-track mind.

Physically he could not have been more unlike the man, for Jackson was so broad and thick across the shoulders that he looked shorter than his bare regulation height of five feet eight. Yet he did not appear to have an ounce of spare flesh anywhere —not on his lean, leathery face or beneath his spade chin or on his massive body. He was hatless, showing close-cut, iron-grey hair—although he was only in his middle thirties.

His handshake was vice-like.

'Glad to know you're interested in this set-up, Mr. Rollison —nasty business.'

They were outside the shop, where several police cars were gathered. Four policemen were keeping would-be customers and those who had come to gape, at bay. Inside the shop, which were quite spacious, photographers and fingerprint men were packing up their materials. The place had been cleaned down, and was almost ready to open again. Only the shelves loomed bare.

At the back of the shop, out of sight, a woman was saying:

'I tell you it's crazy—we've hardly a thing to sell!'

'Then we'll sell what we have, and we can borrow from somewhere else,' a man said stubbornly.

'The Slaters—he wants to re-open, she doesn't,' Jackson said. He was clearly a man who believed in stating the obvious. 'He came back from hospital only twenty minutes ago. He was badly coshed, but no permanent injury. Like to meet them?'

'In a minute,' Grice said. 'Do you need me for anything?'

'I don't think so, sir.'

'Then show us both round and then I'll be off,' said Grice.

Jackson told them all he knew, based on the statements of Jill Slater and two neighbours, described the youths and the small, insignificant car, said that from start to finish the raid appeared to have taken no more than four minutes.

'Has the vehicle been found yet?' asked Grice.

'No. The description's out, of course.'

'Eye-witnesses?'

'Apart from the Slaters, a neighbour and an elderly man at a window of a house opposite,' Jackson answered.

Soon afterwards Grice went off, obviously anxious to get back to his gardening. Once he had gone, something of the formality dropped away from Jackson, who gave a quick, infectious grin, and said:

'Never expected to work with *you*, Mr. Rollison. Like to meet my chaps?' He introduced Rollison to several tall men, all with some curiously indefinable look in common. Rollison's right hand felt as if it had been through a mill when it was over.

Then Jackson took Rollison out into the back room and as the door swung open, Jack Slater was saying:

'They won't come back, and if they do, this time I'll be ready for them.'

Slater was brandishing a gun.

CHAPTER FOUR

JACK SLATER

SLATER stood in the far corner, near a window, with several big cartons behind him. His wife stood by a door leading to the kitchen. Slater looked pale and his eyes glittered; in some ways, he was physically not unlike Jackson, excepting that his brown hair was curly, and his chin less like a spade than a rock.

Jackson became his most formal self.

'I should be careful what you do with that offensive weapon, sir.'

Slater swung round on him.

'That isn't an offensive weapon, it's a defensive one. And if any vicious bloody crook takes a crack at me or my wife again I'll blow his bloody head off with it.'

His wife, distressed, tried to calm him.

'Is the weapon loaded, sir?' inquired Jackson, evenly.

'Yes, it's loaded all right. And if you're not bloody careful this so-called offensive weapon will go off in *your* ear.'

Jackson, looking angry, bit his lip. Jill Slater, hands raised in front of her slender bosom, repeated: '*Jack, don't, please don't.*' Was she cowed, Rollison wondered; was this exhibition characteristic? Or were they both recovering from shock and reacting in different ways?

'So clear your flat-foots out of my shop, or they'll get an offensive weapon up their behinds. *This!*' He swung his right leg through the air and sent an empty cigarette carton flying.

'Must you be so childish?' Rollison asked, coldly.

Slater's eyes swivelled towards him.

'Who the hell are you?'

'I was asked if I would help you.'

'So you're a bloody newspaperman! Well, the same as I'll do to flat-foots I'll do to you if you don't clear out.'

'*Jack!*' cried Jill Slater in a voice suddenly grown strong. 'Put that gun down and behave like a civilised human being.'

Slater glared at her—but there was not the venom in his expression that there had been when talking to the men. 'It's bad enough to have a lot of bullet-headed coppers tramping all over the place but when it comes to a bloody gossip columnist who looks like a——'

Rollison moved.

Chief Inspector Jackson had never seen any man move so fast—nor had Jill. And Slater, although he saw the stranger coming at him, had neither time nor space to move away. He pointed the gun. On that instant an unpleasant situation became ugly and dangerous. Jill stifled a scream, Jackson roared '*Drop that!*' as Rollison pushed the gun aside with one sweep of his arm, swung Slater round, and planted a kick on his buttocks with enough force to send him staggering. The gun dropped from his hand.

At that moment the door opened and a man called:

'You all right, sir?'

'Keep out,' Jackson ordered.

'Very good, sir.' The door closed instantly.

Jill stood breathing hard. Jackson, wary, moved nearer the gun as if afraid that Slater would snatch it up again. Slater, saved from falling by the cartons, straightened up and turned slowly round. Rollison, waiting, expected him to fling himself forward in attack. There was an ugly bruise on his right temple, which showed vivid against the pallor of his skin. On that skin was an old scar—the stitch-marks clearly visible.

Suddenly, Slater grinned.

The grin was broad and infectious, and for the first time, without malice. He dropped his right hand to his thigh and began to rub.

'Well, at least you *do* something, you don't just stand

around and click cameras and sprinkle powder all over the place. *Are* you Press?'

'No,' said Rollison. 'All your guesses about me, so far, have been wrong.'

Slater looked puzzled, then caught the implication and chuckled—so his wits were as quick as his temper.

'I won't argue,' he said.

Jackson moved to the cartons and picked up the Luger; Slater made no attempt to stop him breaking the gun and finding out whether it was loaded. From Jackson's expression and the care with which he handled it, Rollison assumed that it was.

'Have you a licence for this gun?' demanded Jackson, obviously expecting a negative answer.

'Yes,' said Slater.

'You *have*, sir?'

'Yes. Want to see it?'

'If you please.'

Slater hesitated.

Jackson said formally: 'Until you can produce the licence, I'm afraid I shall have to confiscate the gun sir.'

Slater's voice showed a touch of hysteria as he cried wearily: 'No one's going to take it away from me now. When I said I'll blow the head off anyone who breaks into my shop again, I meant it.'

'I've already cautioned you on the dangers of using the weapon,' Jackson said formally. 'Have you anything to add to your original statement?'

'There's nothing to add.'

'What about you, madam?'

'I—I told you everything,' said Jill Slater, much calmer and more poised. 'Have you found them yet?'

'Every effort is being made to apprehend them, ma'am.'

Rollison was beginning to feel irritated by Jackson's ponderous and out-moded way of talking.

'If there is anything at all you remember that might help us in our inquiries,' Jackson went on, 'please advise me at once. I gave you my card.' He cleared his throat. 'This is Mr. Richard Rollison, who has been asked to assist other victims of similar attacks, and has put his services at your disposal. Do you need me any further, Mr. Rollison?'

'I'd like to see a copy of the statements as soon as they're available,' Rollison said.

'I'll see to it, sir.' Jackson, who had obviously been fully briefed by Grice, nodded to each in turn and then went out. Hardly had the door closed than Slater muttered something under his breath, which sounded like: 'Pompous idiot.' Then he caught sight of his wife's face, and said: 'All right, I'll cut it out.' He looked at Rollison with a mixture of impudence and impatience. 'You must be quite somebody for the police to let you in on this. *What* did you say your name was?'

'Rollison. Richard Rollison.'

The girl caught her breath. '*Rollison.*'

Slater glanced at her, frowning, and remarked: 'It rings a bell of some kind. *Rollison.*'

Jill blurted out: '*The Toff!*'

Rollison said mildly: 'That's what some people call me.'

'Well—I'm—damned!' Slater moved slowly across the room, and stood squarely in front of Rollison. 'And I suppose some would say it was an honour to be kicked in the pants by the great Toff!' In spite of the half-mocking way he spoke, he did not seem displeased. 'You wouldn't care to let us in on the secret of *why* you've been brought in, would you?'

'If we could sit somewhere in comfort——' Rollison began.

'You can sit. We've got work to do. Damn it, I forgot to ask that pompous basket whether we could have our shop back.' He picked up a carton marked *Players*, kicked open the door, and staggered through into the shop. The door swung to, into Rollison's face. He backed away and glanced sharply at Jill Slater.

'Does your husband *always* behave like this?'

'No, he——' began Jill, only to hesitate and then say

diffidently: 'Well, he does since his accident. It seems to have made a difference to his outlook. He loses his temper very easily, and if anything upsets him he *is* inclined to be violent—but he doesn't mean it half the time, please don't hold it against him.' She had brushed her hair out of her eyes and they looked quite beautiful.

Rollison smiled. 'I don't. Do you think——'

The door opened again and Slater said: 'Shake a leg, love—we want to get those shelves as full as we can. We're open for business in ten minutes. Don't happen to know of a tobacconist we could get some stocks from, do you?'

Promptly, Rollison said: 'Have you a telephone?'

'Er—yes. You don't mean to say——' Slater broke off, as if unbelieving. 'The telephone's in the shop.'

Two minutes later, Rollison was talking to Jolly.

'. . . and it doesn't matter where it comes from—Ebbutt might be able to help. Fix it, Jolly—a good all round supply . . . I'm sure you will.' He rang off, spun round, and said: 'If we're going to get this shop open in ten minutes, we'll have to hurry. How much stock have you got in this room?'

Dazedly, Slater said: 'Quite a bit.'

'But you mustn't——' began Jill.

Rollison picked up a carton of cigarettes, which was heavier than he had expected, and kicked open the shop door. Almost at once the others followed, and they were piling packets of cigarettes and tobacco up on the shelves when the first of the genuine customers came in. Quite suddenly, Rollison found himself taking money and handing over cigarettes, while Slater brought what stocks they had from next door, and Jill sold sweets to children who seemed to come in droves.

A man asked for twenty Players.

'I'm afraid we're out of stock,' said Rollison regretfully.

'Well—what *have* you got? I'll have those Weights—you seem to have a lot of them.' He took the cigarettes and went off happily, as Rollison heard Jill say:

'We haven't any *coco-chocs* left, I'm afraid.'

'Well,' piped a boy, 'I don't mind what it is so long as it's chocolate.'

In the next half-hour a dozen men and as many children said the same thing ... every other man spoke about the robbery, every woman commiserated. There was hardly a lull during that half-hour, but one came at last, and in the shop there was a strange silence, until Jill began to tidy some of the shelves. Then Slater said in a very subdued voice: 'They didn't mind what they had, so long as they bought something.'

'They seemed to come just for the sake of buying,' Jill said.

Rollison warmed to them more than he had ever hoped to, as he remarked:

'They can be pretty good—people. Most of them, anyway.'

'Just being neighbourly,' Jill said.

As she finished speaking, a van drew up outside, the name *Toby's* painted across it. Rollison, more familiar with the East End than either of the Slater's, realised that first Jolly and then Ebbutt had indeed been busy. This was a delivery of goods from the wholesalers whose trade, concentrated in the East End, spread more or less through the whole of London.

A burly man came in—not in uniform but in his Sunday best.

' 'Allo, Mr. Ar!' he said. 'Fancy seeing you. Case you don't know me, I'm Bert Williams, driver for Toby's. Bill Ebbutt said there'd been a bit of a do out here and some stock was needed. 'Ad me van loaded up for tomorrer so I thought I might as well do me good deed for the day. Now—what do you want? Pretty well everything, I should say.'

Slater was gaping.

Jill leaned back against the wall and, very quietly, began to cry.

It was half-past seven when the Slaters closed and bolted the shop door. Jill looked exhausted, ready to drop, Jack had sweat on his forehead and lips, his collar was rumpled and discoloured from sweat, the bruise on his forehead was turning an ugly blue.

Rollison had never felt more leg-weary after the fiercest game of Rugby or the longest walk. He was in his shirt-sleeves, and he leaned against the counter, wiping his forehead. The shop was nearly clear of stock again, but this time the shelves were tidy; and this time the till overflowed. The ting-ting-ting of it seemed still to echo in Rollison's ears. Slater moved, with an effort, and put two or three oddments straight, then said:

'We must have taken nearly a hundred pounds.'

'We'll have to take the money to the night safe,' Jill said. 'So it will have to be counted.'

They looked at one another.

'Well, we'll have some supper first,' said Slater—and then for the first time seemed to feel a touch of embarrassment. 'Er—it'll just be a cold snack, Mr. Rollison, but you'll be very welcome.'

'So will a cold snack,' said Rollison, warmly.

Slater's doubts vanished, he straightened up and clapped his hands together . . .

And then a strange thing happened.

A car drew up outside, very slowly. Slater's whole body went tense, so did Jill's. The car was very similar to the one in which the thieves had escaped—and obviously it had a sinister significance for them both. In that moment Rollison realised just how much on edge they were, how deep was the injury caused by the raid.

'Nothing to worry about,' he said. 'That's my man, Jolly.'

As he spoke a man in his sixties, dressed in dark and formal clothes, got out of the car, and moved to the back of it.

'Now what's he up to?' Rollison asked himself *sotto voce*, and took long strides towards the door.

CHAPTER FIVE

PICNIC

As Rollison stepped into the street, the Slaters on his heels, Jolly turned round, carrying what was to Rollison a familiar sight—a big wicker hamper. In that moment understanding dawned. Jolly caught sight of him and smiled. The smile did not make him look a picture of joy, for he was by all standards a glum-looking man, with a lined face and doleful brown eyes, dewlaps, and a rather scraggy neck. Yet there was something warming about his smile as well as in his presence.

'Good evening, sir.'

'Hallo, Jolly! What's the hamper for? More stock?'

'No, indeed, sir,' said Jolly. 'I understood that plenty of supplies had been left here, but it occurred to me that as you had been so busy, there had been no time to arrange a meal. With that in mind, I prepared a picnic, sir.'

Slater asked in a faint voice: 'What is this? Do-your-neighbour-a-good-turn week?'

'Jack—take the hamper!' cried Jill.

'No need at all, madam,' Jolly assured her. 'If you would be kind enough to open the door——' he marched through carrying the hamper as if he were heading a triumphant procession. Jill dashed to lift the flap in the counter as he passed through into the back room.

'It's in a terrible mess,' gasped Jill.

'Nothing a few minutes' work won't straighten,' said Jolly. 'Shall I take this upstairs?'

'Yes, of course!' Jill flew to the stairs, and Jolly followed much more sedately. The sound of his voice floated downwards. 'If you would care to take a tray downstairs, madam, I will heat the soup, and ...'

There was a discussion for perhaps two minutes. Then Jill came downstairs with a tray of chilled lager, glasses, and a bottle of sherry, while Jolly's footsteps sounded upstairs. Very soon they were sitting about the room above the shop, eating cold chicken, ham and tongue, game pie, French bread spread thickly with butter, cheese and fruit salad and cream. Jolly hovered like a ministering angel, Rollison discovered how hungry he was, and the others seemed as if they had not had a square meal for weeks.

At last it was over.

Jolly went downstairs with the empty hamper.

'Mr. Rollison,' Jill Slater said, 'we will never be able to thank you. *Never.*'

'I echo that sentiment,' Slater said gruffly.

Rollison looked from one to the other, and said quietly: 'You never know. You never know.'

'If there's anything at all——' said Jill swiftly.

'Just say the word!' cried Slater.

Rollison shook his head slowly.

'Nothing at all for me, but—— Forget it, for now. An idea passed through my mind, that's all.'

'What kind of idea?' Jill persisted.

'I believe you're the last victim to date of the Golden-haired Boy,' said Rollison. 'Now if you could find a way of getting together with the previous victims, who knows what might happen?' He gave a short laugh. 'I know, I'm being very vague, but I feel vague. Do you want any help counting that money?'

'No, of course not,' Jill answered quickly.

'Two of Mr. Ebbutt's men are outside and will escort Mr. and Mrs. Slater to the bank for the night safe,' Jolly said. 'May I recommend that you come back with me now, sir?'

'What made you appear so opportunely with the hamper?' Rollison asked Jolly.

They were back at Gresham Terrace, and Rollison was relaxing with a brandy in one hand and a cigar in the other. He wore a royal blue silk dressing gown with a fleur-de-lys motif: a present from another aunt. His legs still ached with the unfamiliar exercise, and he had a pleasing sense of well-being; of a job well done.

'Ebbutt arranged for someone to look in and buy something every ten minutes or so,' Jolly answered. 'And when he reported that customers were coming in a constant stream, it was obvious to me that you would need a meal. You had *very* little lunch today,' he added reprovingly.

'Quite a Father Christmas act, and more than appreciated. What else have you been up to?'

'Making tentative inquiries, sir.'

'With what result?' asked Rollison, and motioned to a chair. Jolly sat down, at ease, but not demonstrably so.

'Thank you, sir. Virtually no result except——'

'Yes?'

'Bewilderment.'

'Because Golden Boy is so bold and the police can't put a finger on him.'

'Exactly, sir,' said Jolly. 'And also——' he paused, but Rollison did not prompt him. 'And also, the comparatively *modest* sums the thieves acquire. As I understand it, the value of the stolen goods in each case is an average of three hundred pounds. On resale it is most unlikely that they would get more than one third from any buyer. There are always five men involved, they take grave risks, and they get no more than twenty pounds each.'

'Hardly a living wage,' Rollison said thoughtfully.

'Certainly not worth a risk by normal standards,' reasoned Jolly.

'How many thefts have you on your list?'

'The figure is given as "about twenty".'

'Add Grice's five outside of the East End,' Rollison remarked. 'They may also commit other crimes we know nothing about.' After a long pause, he added: 'And Golden Boy is always involved?'

'*Always,* sir. There is no certainty about the others, they may be the same or they may not.'

'We need to find out,' said Rollison.

'Did Mr. Grice explain why they have had such difficulty?'

'No. But he's worried. He keeps an eye on it himself, and Chief Inspector Jackson is giving most of his time to it. Remember Jackson?'

'The officer who talks like a deposition in the witness box?'

Rollison chuckled.

'You obviously know Jackson. Jolly.'

'Sir?'

'Twenty pounds each, for such a risk, makes no sense at all.'

'I fully agree.'

'So—it might be the means to a more profitable racket.'

'Yes indeed.'

'What else could it be?' Rollison asked.

'I haven't yet thought of any other explanation, sir, except possibly—devilry for the sake of it.'

'*Ah,*' said Rollison heavily. 'So you've seen that.'

'One *has* to consider it, sir, but——' Jolly broke off.

'Not a nice thought,' Rollison said. 'A small gang of cold-blooded young devils putting the fear of God into the old and helpless. Would that be enough satisfaction, do you think?'

'It could be, sir, but—I am never convinced by arguments for motiveless crime. They may *enjoy* what they do but unless they also profit by it——' Jolly broke off. 'I confess that I am very puzzled indeed, sir.'

Rollison said: 'So am I.' After a pause, he went on: 'Didn't you get anything else from Ebbutt?'

'Not positive things, sir.'

'What negative ones?'

'Three of the shopkeepers concerned have been put out of

business,' Jolly told him, 'and two others will probably have to give up. In most of these small shops the margin between profit and loss is fairly small. The shopkeepers buy at comparatively high prices as they buy in such small quantities.'

'You've certainly been probing,' Rollison said. 'It's still true that one half of the world doesn't know how the other half lives, isn't it?' he added sententiously. 'Did Ebbutt suggest anything we could do?'

'No sir—but he very much hopes *you* will think of something, sir.'

Rollison grunted, glanced at his watch, and immediately turned towards a television set in a corner.

'We'll have the late news,' he said, as if he had tired of discussing the robberies.

But after the news, which was not even slightly momentous, and as he stood up to go to bed, he asked almost casually:

'What is happening to the shops which are closed, Jolly?'

'I understand they're to be put up for sale,' said Jolly.

'As going concerns?'

'I didn't go into that, sir.'

'If we're looking for a motive, we must,' Rollison said. 'Goodnight.'

'Goodnight, sir,' Jolly said.

Rollison retired with a book of Browning's poems, the latest sex novel, and the thick Sunday newspapers, but could not concentrate, no matter which he tried to read. Strangely enough it was the sight of Jill Slater crying silently which most affected him. Shock, of course, and yet—strange that she should have been so overcome by the simple kindliness of neighbours.

He put down Browning; put out the light; turned over on his side—and then started up as if he had been shot!

There was an almost deafening noise of smashing glass.

He flung back the bedclothes and jumped out of bed, opening his door as Jolly, pyjama-clad, rushed past in his bare feet.

'*Slippers!*' roared Rollison.

Jolly pulled up as if he had put on a brake.

'I beg your pardon?'

'There's broken glass,' Rollison said, pushing his feet into leather slippers. Jolly glared towards the living-room and they stood still, half-expecting another smash. Instead, they heard the roar of a car engine on the road outside. Rollison sprang forward and switched on the light. The room was a shambles, the floor covered with broken glass—and there was a huge hole in each window, with jagged glass at the edges. Gingerly, he put his head through one of the holes—in time to see a small station wagon turn the corner towards Piccadilly.

As the rear lights disappeared, a light went on at a window opposite and a man shouted:

'Anything the matter over there?'

Rollison called back: 'Some idiot's been throwing stones.'

The man at the other window seemed startled, but after a moment called across:

'Need any help?'

'No, thanks.'

'Better send for the police, eh?'

'Doesn't seem to be that important,' Rollison called, not liking the thought of the police coming here in force at this hour. Once he called them they would undoubtedly make a thorough search. If the neighbour insisted it would be difficult to refuse.

'Your pigeon,' the man called back. 'Goodnight.'

'Goodnight!'

The other closed his window and a moment later the light went out. None other appeared, no one else had heard or, if they had, intended to take any notice. A car turned into the street and pulled up a few doors away; almost at once a long-legged girl climbed out of it, called out: '*Must fly, darling!*' and ran into a house. The car went off almost at once.

Rollison turned round, to see Jolly straightening up with something in his hand. It was a ball—a heavy ball of the type widely used as an imitation cricket ball. Rollison trod on a piece of glass and it cracked sharply, as he moved towards it.

'Is there another?' he asked.

'I believe it's under the desk, sir.' Jolly moved gingerly about the room, bent down, and groped beneath the desk; another ball, identical to the first, rolled out.

Rollison weighed it in his hand as he surveyed the damage. Several of the trophies had been shaken from their places on the wall, but none appeared to be damaged. Two ash-trays were on the floor and a fragile Venetian bowl lay in smithereens in the fireplace.

Rollison said reflectively: 'The chap can throw.'

'It's a long way from the street, sir.'

'Yes. And he scored two direct hits. It looks as if they are now trying to scare us off,' mused Rollison. 'And not simply for the sadistic pleasure they hope to get out of it.' He tossed the ball from hand to hand again. 'Obtainable at any sports shop,' he remarked. 'But not on Sunday night.'

'Meaning what, sir?'

'Someone had them at hand—didn't go out to buy them. That could help us, Jolly.' After a pause, he went on: 'The mess can wait until the morning, but we ought to do something about the windows, I suppose.'

'I've a roll of clearex. If I pin pieces up at the window and then draw the curtains, that should be sufficient,' said Jolly. 'There is no need for you to stay up, sir.'

'I'll lend you a hand,' Rollison said, and as his man demurred and he wondered whether the issue was worth forcing, the telephone bell rang.

It was exactly a quarter to one.

CHAPTER SIX

GOLDEN VOICE

ROLLISON moved slowly to the big desk while Jolly, crunching glass underfoot, hurried to the extension in the kitchen. The bell kept ringing. Rollison deliberately took his time, but at last lifted the receiver.

'Who's that?' he barked.

'Who is *that*?' asked a man with a most attractive voice.

On the instant, Rollison thought of the golden-haired youth and all he had heard of him; and he kept silent. There was a faint laugh at the other end of the line, and the voice went on:

'Are you getting tired, Mr. Rollison?'

Rollison said coolly: 'My patience is certainly not inexhaustible. Exactly what do you want?'

'Your co-operation,' the speaker said.

'In what?'

'In my little pastime. I don't want to tangle with you but if you don't mind your own business you'll get hurt.'

'Ah,' said Rollison. 'You enjoy hurting people, don't you?'

'It's one of my life's pleasures,' the other retorted.

'So I supposed. And one of mine will be to cut those charming locks,' Rollison said.

He heard the other catch his breath, had a fleeting thought that the youth was sensitive about his hair—and was then assailed by a stream of obscenities and vituperation which at first startled, then disgusted, and finally appalled him. He held the receiver away from his ear, was about to put it down when he heard something very clearly:

'... and I'm warning you, neither you or that stuffed dummy who works for you will see the day out.'

Very slowly, shocked by what he had heard and by the malevolence in the once pleasant-sounding voice, Rollison replaced the receiver. He felt cold—icy cold. He heard sounds in the other room, and Jolly appeared. Was it imagination, or did Jolly look shaken?

'Not a pleasant personality,' Rollison remarked.

Slowly, Jolly said: 'I think we should be *very* careful, sir.'

'So he impressed you like that, did he?' After a pause, Rollison went on: 'What have we struck, Jolly?'

'He sounded almost—insane, sir.'

'Yes. Yes, he certainly did,' agreed Rollison. 'And very proud of his hair. Jolly——'

'Sir?'

'A list of East End hairdressers and the names of youths with golden hair who habitually attend them, might help us. And Jolly,' went on Rollison, 'I think we can keep an open mind about motive. This chap may simply hate.'

'*Would* he endeavour to frighten us off the affair simply for that, sir?' asked Jolly. 'I am inclined to think he was incensed at being crossed.'

Rollison shrugged, and then went to his bedroom, no longer insisting on lending a helping hand. He heard Jolly moving about, then heard his door close. It was half-past one, but at least they could now get some sleep.

He was dozing when the telephone at his bedside rang, insistently enough to make him start up in bed. The main instrument in the living-room was ringing, too. He took off the receiver rather gingerly, fearful of what he might hear.

'Richard Rollison,' he said.

An ear-splitting whistle sounded on the telephone, making him snatch it away from his ear. The whistle went on and on, until he replaced the receiver. As he did so the door opened and Jolly asked:

'What was that, sir?'

'Our friend,' said Rollison slowly. His head was ringing

from that piercing sound; nothing could have been more calculated to cause alarm and discomfort. 'If that happens often——'

The telephone bell rang again. He looked at it, without moving. Jolly drew further into the room but was no more anxious to answer. At last Rollison lifted the receiver cautiously and kept it inches from his ear.

'Richard Rollison,' he said.

'You're going to die today,' said the youth with the golden voice, and he rang off before Rollison could say a word.

A quarter of an hour later Rollison put out the light again, and tried to settle down, but he was wide awake. Worse: he was on edge in case the telephone should shrill out again, that charming voice still ringing in his ears as it uttered words both prophetic and sinister:

'You're going to die today.'

Most of his life Rollison had been familiar with threats; with vicious men; with danger. He had never felt quite so edgy as he did now.

But at last he went to sleep.

He woke, to broad daylight, with a sense of foreboding which did not clear when he realised what had caused it. He tried to reason with himself, that threats were ten-a-penny, that the youth had simply meant to unnerve and frighten him, but he was not wholly convinced. He *had* to laugh it off, of course, but he certainly mustn't be careless today.

There was a tap at the door.

'Come in, Jolly,' he called, slightly puzzled because Jolly's usual practice when bringing him his morning tea was to enter without knocking. He eased himself up in bed, as the door opened slowly. That was unusual, too, Jolly normally opened it firmly. There was no clinking of cup and saucer, either, Jolly's favourite device to make him wake.

Suddenly, he thought: *My God!*

He flung himself from the bed, on the side away from the

door, as it opened swiftly and a man tossed something on to the bed.

Rollison just saw the man—or rather, youth—hurling the missile as he dropped from the bed to the floor. His fall coincided with a sharp hiss of sound and then an explosion which rocked the bed and the room. The door slammed, there was a thudding of footsteps and the slamming of another door.

And there was the sudden pungent odour of burning.

It had happened so swiftly that even as he recognised the smell, Rollison was in a daze from the heavy fall from the bed. He thought: *Jolly, where's Jolly?* and then saw a streak of fire—the clothes were aflame. He rolled beneath the bed and out the other side. The mattress and the pillows, where his head would have been, were blazing furiously and there were a dozen fires—something like a petrol bomb had been flung. *Jolly, where's Jolly?* he wondered fearfully as he leapt up and sprang towards the door. At the last moment, he paused; if he opened it swiftly it could cause a draught which would fan the flames to greater height. There was an extinguisher in the kitchen but whether an extinguisher was enough to put this blaze out seemed doubtful. He opened the door cautiously, then went to the kitchen; there was no sign of Jolly. He took the extinguisher off the hook, knocked the cap off as he went back to the bedroom, then thumbed the plunger. A stream of evil-smelling foam shot out and instantly the flames died at the foot of the bed, but one side of the room was still ablaze. *Where was Jolly?* He kept up a steady stream of the foam and gradually the fire was driven back.

The jet dried up.

He must get water.

As he ran out of the room again, still feeling the heat behind him, he saw Jolly getting slowly on to his knees, fumbling at the latch of the front door. There was a deep cut at the side of his face. Then, with blessed relief, he saw the front door swing open and a policeman step through.

'Is there——' the man began.

'Dial fire,' breathed Rollison. 'Then come and help me.'

Instead of dialling anything, the policeman took a walkie-talkie radio from his pocket and spoke into it. Thankfulness swept over Rollison. Help would be here in a few minutes, now. But there were huge clouds of smoke billowing from his bedroom, he must get that water.

He was spraying water from a bucket over the nearer fire when the policeman joined him, and almost at once a neighbour appeared with another extinguisher. A second policeman arrived as a siren screeched, reminding him of the piercing whistle on the telephone.

Then a woman said: 'You really ought to come and sit down, Mr. Rollison.' He recognised her, middle-aged and comely, from the flat below. 'Everything will be all right now. *Please* come and sit down.'

Sit down? He felt like falling down.

'Good of you,' he muttered, and then alarm flared again. *Jolly*. He looked almost desperately about him as he was led into the living-room.

Jolly was sitting in his, Rollison's, chair while a man pressed a pad of some kind over the cut in his head. Jolly, obviously in pain, nevertheless kept looking about him; then he saw Rollison, and appeared to relax.

Soon, firemen arrived; then an ambulance, and under protest Jolly was taken off in it, able to walk but undoubtedly in need of bandages and plaster, if not of stitches. Rollison took refuge in the small dining-alcove, still bemused by the speed of events as well as shaken by what had happened.

'You are going to die today,' the gentle-voiced youth had menaced.

And he had already been within an ace of death.

With firemen and police trampling all over the flat, Rollison stayed in the alcove, guarded and ministered to by the neighbour who had come upstairs. She was speaking, now, to someone at the door, and he heard her say:

'There really isn't anything he can do ... I think he should rest.'

'He can rest after I've seen him,' said Superintendent Grice, striding forward. The neighbour, annoyed, stood to one side. Grice, a head taller, looked down on Rollison, and there was no particular friendliness in his voice. 'You are a fool,' he announced.

'Tell me some other time,' Rollison protested.

'This really shouldn't be permitted,' the neighbour protested.

'I don't wish to be rude, madam,' Grice said, 'but this is a police matter and I do know what I'm doing.' He turned back to Rollison, and went on: 'I've talked to a man opposite who said you had some trouble last night but didn't think it worthwhile calling us.'

Rollison drew a deep breath.

'You're absolutely right,' he said. 'I was a fool. Several other things happened last night, too. I will tell you.' He began to talk, feeling much more himself, and he saw the amazement on his neighbour's face as she stood listening. He left nothing out—not even the way the threat had affected him. Even now he seemed to be able to hear that charming voice over the telephone.

'You ought to have had a police guard, back and front,' Grice said.

'Yes, Bill. Better late than never. Will you arrange it?'

'If it will help,' promised Grice, 'although you aren't going to be able to stay here, are you?'

Rollison looked round the room, hearing the men moving about the flat, and realised that Grice was right. So he had another problem: where to live. Very tentatively, the woman said:

'I have a spare room, Mr. Rollison.'

'You're very good,' said Rollison, 'but I should hate anything like this to happen to you. My club will probably be safer, too, both for me and for Jolly.' It occurred to him that he was taking the woman's offer very casually, and he turned to her with much more feeling in his voice. 'You've been extraordinarily good already.'

She flushed with pleasure . . .

When she had gone, Grice spoke in a less censorious but still critical voice:

'You won't keep anything like this from us again, will you?'

'No,' Rollison said; and then forced the first grin he had felt able to achieve since the moment of understanding. 'Not if I continue to feel as I do at the moment. Bill——'

'Yes?'

'*You* haven't been keeping anything back, have you?'

Grice almost laughed.

'No. What did you think I might have kept back?'

'Knowledge of how dangerous this is,' said Rollison.

'I told you everything I knew about it,' Grice assured him. 'I know a lot more now. Do you say he seemed to lose his self-control the moment you said you would dock his hair?'

'That's how it seemed to me,' Rollison said. They were silent for a few moments, and then he went on: 'If this can be as ugly as it is for me, what about the Slaters. Are you having their shop watched?'

'Yes,' said Grice. 'Not that I've reason to believe they're in danger. You're the one I'm worried about. From the sound of Golden Boy, he doesn't like being thwarted. There might be another attempt to kill you very soon. Know what I think, Rolly?'

Rollison looked at him steadily, almost owlishly, and then said:

'No, Bill. What do you think?'

'You ought to withdraw from this case while you're still alive,' Grice said.

CHAPTER SEVEN

ADVICE FROM A FRIEND

ROLLISON sat very still.

Until that moment he had been in a kind of daze; shocked by what had happened, worried for Jolly, confused by the way in which the police and firemen had taken over. Even the fact that he would have to move until the flat was made habitable again had not made a deep impression on his mind, he hadn't realised its full significance.

Grice's words acted like a douche of icy water.

This man from the Yard, Rollison's oldest friend there, never said what he did not mean; he was the most forthright man Rollison knew. Now he was grim-faced and firm-voiced, and his gaze did not waver for an instant.

There had been a time when this would have meant: 'Get out of our hair—we don't want you interfering.'

It did not mean that now; it meant that Grice had come to the conclusion that he, Rollison, would be *killed* if he continued with the case of the shopkeeper victims.

How long he sat there, not responding, he did not know. The bustle went on about him, the neighbour—why on earth couldn't he remember her name?—was hovering; and at last Grice stirred and spoke again.

'Take advice from an old friend,' he said.

'Yes,' Rollison said gruffly. 'It's advice and it's from an old friend.' He looked and sounded shocked. 'Bill—answer this again, will you?'

'Answer what?'

'*Do* you know more about this case than you've told me?'

'I do not.'

'Then, why——'

'Now don't be a fool,' said Grice, sharply. 'You don't need *more* telling that it's deadly. I've been uneasy about it for a long time. This youth—for we assume it was he who telephoned you—has all the signs of a psychopathic killer. He doesn't get much money out of it. He's vicious. He obviously gets satisfaction out of terrifying helpless people——'

'Would you call young Slater helpless?' demurred Rollison, pleased at this small sign that his mind was beginning to work again.

'Taken at a disadvantage like that, anyone is virtually helpless,' argued Grice. 'There isn't much doubt of the vicious pleasure Golden Boy derives from these attacks, is there?'

'No. Sadistic is the word.'

'Golden Boy's never really been crossed before,' Grice said. 'I've wondered what would happen if he were—I didn't like the indications.'

'That he'd kill?'

'That he would behave like a psychopath,' Grice stated flatly. 'You didn't actually interfere with him, you just put right something he'd done. And—he intends to kill you.'

Rollison gave a little involuntary shudder.

'How would he know I'd done that?' he asked.

'A dozen people could have told him,' answered Grice. 'Ebbutt's men kept going in and out of the Slater shop, and they would talk—no reason why they shouldn't. Now, Golden Boy is determined to make sure you can't interfere again. Anyone who works the East End knows what you're capable of doing, Rolly.'

Rollison said owlishly:

'Cut me down before I can do any harm.'

'Obviously.'

'And you think that I should back out—so that I can't possibly do him any harm,' Rollison said heavily.

Grice hitched himself up in his chair, squared his shoulders, and looked very straightly into Rollison's eyes. He did not speak at once, and the delay made his manner the more impressive.

'Rolly,' he said, 'this youth has done you more harm in a matter of minutes than any of the vicious criminals you've fought over twenty *years*. This flat is a shambles. Jolly's in hospital—and even if he's let out soon, he won't be able to do much. You—*you* look as nearly out on your feet as I've known you. These are *facts*. Don't ignore them. In one blow, Golden Boy has halved—even quartered—your effectiveness.'

Rollison gulped.

'So it seems.'

Grice relaxed a little—and then did a rare thing for him: he stretched out a hand and gripped Rollison's arm for a moment; and his grip was very firm. Rollison almost held his breath for what was to come next.

'Rolly,' Grice said, 'I don't want you to die. I——' he hesitated, groping for suitable words. 'I haven't had much chance of telling you what I've come to think of you. It's a long time since I first met you, and thought you the most bumptious and arrogant young man I'd ever met. The first two or three cases you helped with, I put down to luck. You always had courage and you used it to back your luck. But——' he drew a deep breath. 'It didn't take me long to realise the truth, that you had a quality *I'd* never met in a human being. That if you believed a thing right you went ahead and did it whether *I* approved, or the Yard approved, or whether you were likely to get your throat cut in the bargain. And——'

'Er——' began Rollison, coming slowly out of the amazement which Grice in such a mood created.

'Don't interrupt!' rasped Grice. 'And you've never made a penny out of it. Whenever you could you've dodged the limelight. I have a dozen cases to my credit which were nothing to do with me. You solved them—some of them in the face of my bitter opposition—and handed them to me on a plate. All these years I've taken them, and I can't recall that I've ever thanked you.'

'Now, Bill——' Rollison began again.

'Be quiet! Instead of thanking you I've been sour and bloody-minded—told you that *you* got away with it this time, but if you try again I'll have your neck. That's the *truth* of it,' went on Grice, and it was easy to believe that his anger and impatience were directed at himself. 'What's more—this has been the attitude of most of the senior men at the Yard. "What's Rollison been up to now?" they ask. "When are we going to get him out of our hair?" instead of "Thank God Rollison can cut across red tape and regulations when our hands are tied." Instead of hounding you, we should plead with you to help us.'

'Bill,' Rollison said, firmly, 'this is too much.'

'It's the simple truth,' Grice said. 'And now that I've got it off my chest with you I'll let a few others know what I think.'

'If you——'

'Your one trouble is you can never *listen*!' growled Grice. 'Well, you're going to listen now. It was Marion who started me off last night. I—well, if you must know,' he went on as if under pressure from Rollison, 'she asked me whether I realised how much I admired and respected you. With a wife's bluntness, she told me that everything I *say* is anti-Toff and everything I *do* is pro-Toff. And that's about it. Last night——' Grice jumped to his feet and began to pace the room, glass crunching under his feet. 'Last night, I showed her how worried I was about you. I don't know why it is, but this case gets under my skin. I feel as if we're dealing with forces we can't see or understand. That sound melodramatic to you?' he demanded aggressively.

'Not at all,' Rollison said humbly.

'And I don't want to lose *you*.'

'I don't want to be lost,' said Rollison, who felt a strange, almost exhilarating sense of well-being—induced not only by Grice's words but by the near-passion with which he uttered them.

'Then drop the case,' Grice said.

'And give Golden Boy a bloodless victory?'

'He won't win, in the long run. But he could do a lot of damage during the chase.'

'If he drives me out,' Rollison remarked, 'it might unleash more of those unknown forces you talk about.'

'Rolly,' Grice said, coming to a standstill squarely in front of the chair, 'you've won case after case, year in year out. Because you've held on longer than the other chaps, you've never had a real failure. Don't let pride in the record keep you going when you should drop out. These modern criminals are twenty-five years younger than you are. They've got the strength and staying power and know-how you haven't. It's time you stopped, Rolly—and this is the case to stop at.'

Rollison looked at him without speaking.

'Will you drop this case before any more harm is done?' demanded Grice.

'I will not,' said Rollison, with great deliberation.

Of course, Grice had expected it. He was disappointed and exasperated, but he did not try to force the issue any further. Probably he was suffering reaction from his own outburst— and from the measure of feeling he had allowed himself to show. He turned round and appeared to become aware that others were still about, though none within earshot; then swung sharply back on Rollison.

'At least, think about it.'

'Yes. I'll think about it.'

'And don't try to do too much on your own. We can help with practically everything, this time.'

'I won't stick my neck out.'

Grice looked at him steadily for what seemed a long time, and then a faint smile curved his lips. Without speaking, he turned away and went to see what the firemen were doing. Rollison was alone, but on his feet and feeling very much more himself, when he heard scurrying footsteps on the stairs—not those of a policeman or a fireman. And without any warning or cause, his heart began to beat fast with something not far removed from fear. The front door was open, at least one policeman was on duty there. Whoever was coming up had the spring of youth in his step.

'Good morning, sir.' That was a policeman, stolidly.

'I must see Mr. Rollison,' a young man cried. '*Is he all right?*'

It was Jack Slater, his voice at its most insistent, just as it had been when he had rounded on Jackson and then the Toff.

Rollison moved forward, surprised at the measure of his relief.

'Want me, young Slater?' he called.

He saw through the big room into the entrance hall and to the door, where Jack Slater was parleying with the policeman, looking both fierce and angry.

Then he saw Rollison, and pulled up in his tracks.

He said: 'They told me you were dead,' in a flat voice, that carried with it shock and disquiet.

His words, in their implication, stressed so meaningly what Grice had been saying. They went further. Slater had felt a conviction—that he, the Toff, was dead; and to feel such a conviction he must have been deeply concerned.

Rollison said: 'They certainly tried to kill me.'

'Are you——' Slater's voice was gruff. 'Are you all right?'

'The only damage is superficial,' Rollison said.

Slater stared hard at Rollison, and then in a slightly easier voice said:

'How's Mr. Jolly?'

'Injured but not seriously.'

'Thank God for that,' said Slater. There was a lightening of his tone and a gleam of humour in his eyes when he went on: 'Does your telephone still work in this mess?'

'Yes.'

'May I make a call? ... Thanks ... Over there?' Slater

strode across the room, picked up the receiver and dialled, drummed his fingers impatiently on the dust-covered desk, and then said eagerly: 'Jill ... He's all right ... Yes, I can see him from where I'm standing! ... Jolly's been hurt but he's okay ... No, I won't be long, 'bye sweetie.' He put the receiver down with a bang, clapped his hands together, turned to Rollison, and said: 'She was worried out of her wits, never known her so interested in the fate of a man.'

'She mustn't waste her sympathy on me,' Rollison said, but his heart warmed. 'Who told you I was dead?'

'Two men telephoned,' answered Slater. 'One was that smooth devil with the honey in his voice, the other was just somebody. They both said the same thing.' Slater paused, his expression assuming the blankness of a man who is recalling the words of another. 'They just said: "Nobody gets in *my* way. Rollison's dead." And then rang off. Mr. Rollison,' went on Slater very slowly, 'what's going on? What *is* it all about?'

'That's what we're going to find out,' Rollison said.

'What can *I* do?'

'Give me a chance to get over this crisis, and we'll talk about it,' Rollison said. 'Meanwhile, be very careful, and don't take any chances with Jill. She's too nice to be hurt.'

Very heavily, Slater said: 'If anyone hurts her, I'll break his neck.'

But he was in a brighter mood when he left, a few minutes afterwards.

Rollison and Grice made a quick tour of the flat, and the first thing Rollison realised was that the damage to his bedroom had been much greater than he had supposed. There wasn't a suit undamaged, hardly a pair of shoes. A cabinet with socks and shirts and accessories had remained untouched, and the bathroom door had been closed, limiting the destruction, but otherwise he had no clothes.

Jolly's room was hardly damaged.

'I've checked with the hospital,' Grice said. 'He's comfortable and not on the danger list but they think he'll be there for a week. He told our man that he simply opened the door to a ring, and was attacked. Savage young devils, these people.'

'Yes,' said Rollison, sombrely. 'Savage young devils, indeed. We're going to have to civilise them, Bill.'

'I suppose it always was a waste of time expecting you to go off the case,' Grice said. 'I wish I didn't feel as sure as I do that you should.'

CHAPTER EIGHT

'IF AT FIRST YOU DON'T SUCCEED . . .'

ROLLISON watched Grice leave, with those last words ringing in his ears. There was little to be cheerful about—except, possibly, one thing. Alone, he took keys from his desk, went back to his bedroom, and opened the drawer in the bottom of the main wardrobe. Beneath some folded linen and casual wear was a secret section, and he pressed an almost invisible spot in one side of the drawer. The partition slid open. There, carefully stored, were his weapons.

There were two automatics; loaded.

There was a palm gun, so small that it could be fastened to the palm of the hand, and so cleverly covered that it looked like part of the hand.

There was a small gas pistol.

There was a case of cigarettes loaded with pellets which, blown from the cigarettes, could put a man out for hours.

There were knives fastened to clips—like bracelets—which fitted his arm and his leg and which could be released simply by flexing his muscles. There were knock-out drops, and a small malacca cane, which was in fact a sword stick.

All these weapons the Toff had acquired over the years.

There were times when he saw film and television extravaganzas and read lightly spiced and furious-paced books where he read that this hero or that, from Bond to U.N.C.L.E., had 'invented' the remarkable weapons which they used . . . and there, in this drawer, was the prototype of practically every one of them.

The drawer could be pulled out and put into an ordinary suitcase, itself self-locking and impregnable.

He moved the drawer, locked the case, and placed it in the passage for all to see. Then he packed another case, missing Jolly and being anxious for him. Next, he rummaged in Jolly's room and found two dry cleaners' receipts for suits—one grey, one brown; so the problem of clothes was solved. He packed yet a third case of essentials for Jolly, then went back into the main room.

Jackson, vast, and seemingly impregnable, was studying the Trophy Wall. He turned to survey Rollison with that unexpectedly broad smile.

'Quite a collection, sir.'

'I can't wait to add a golden wig to it,' Rollison said.

The smile disappeared.

'Think it's a wig, sir?'

'Think it could be.'

'That's against the evidence,' stated Jackson, very formally.

'Against the apparent evidence,' Rollison said.

'No doubt we'll find out in time,' said Jackson. 'I'm very sorry about this, sir.'

'Thank you.'

'I've just come from Jolly,' Jackson stated. 'I am glad to inform you that his condition is not likely to deteriorate. He asks me to convey his esteem, sir.'

'*Esteem?*' echoed Rollison.

'His exact word,' Jackson assured him.

Rollison smiled. 'Get any description from him?'

'He hardly glimpsed his assailant, but it was not the youth known as Golden Boy,' announced Jackson.

'Pity.'

'Yes indeed, sir. What are your immediate plans?'

Before Rollison could answer, there was a bellow from below—the unmistakable bull-like roar emitted by Bill Ebbutt when emotion overcame wheeziness.

'Don't you tell *me* I can't go up and see the Toff, I'll knock your bloody block off!' There was a sound which might have been a scuffle, and then heavy footsteps on the stairs; Ebbutt was on his way. Soon, he appeared—and in exactly the same way as Jack Slater, he espied the Toff and stood stockstill.

Then, huskily, he said: 'I knew it was a lie.'

'What was a lie, Bill?' asked Rollison, but he was already aware of the answer.

'Some type telephoned and told me you were dead,' he said. 'All over the East End it is—can't turn around without hearing it. Do you know what *I* said?' demanded Ebbutt, coming forward and gripping Rollison's hand tightly. 'I said it was a lie, you hadn't had your nine lives yet by a long way, but if it *was* true then you were going to have the biggest bloody funeral we've had in the East End since old Sir Reggie died.'

Rollison stared.

Jackson stared.

Then suddenly they all burst out laughing, Ebbutt coming in a little behind the others, his guffaw drowning them both as soon as he was in full spate.

At last, they settled down.

And soon Rollison was on his way to his club, sitting high by Ebbutt's side in the sky-blue Model T Ford which turned every eye in London except—inevitably—the eye of the chief doorman of the Carilon Club, a tall and formidable man. He and Ebbutt, in fact, were much of a size,

'... and don't forget, Mr. Ar,' Ebbutt was saying as they stopped, 'there will always be two of my chaps on duty, night and day. It will take four of them to make up for Jolly but they'll do their best. They'll each have a car handy—use them any way you want, Mr. Ar.'

'You're very good,' Rollison said humbly.

'Least we can do,' said Ebbutt. 'Put the perishing wind up me it did, when they said you was dead. You'll be careful, now?'

'Very careful, Bill.'

'Don't want to lose you, you know,' remarked Ebbutt. 'And these perishers—there's something about this case I don't like—can't put a finger on it but—it's not just *crime*, if you see what I mean. There's something nasty going on.'

So everyone felt it.

Something nasty; savage; psychopathic; primitive … in the Golden Boy.

Rollison shivered.

As he was going to stay for a week or two, he was given a room high over the pleasance of St. James's Park; he could see the lakes and the flower beds, the masses of people and the smooth lawns, and above them the new sky-line of London and even Big Ben. If he leaned out of the window far enough he could see Buckingham Palace. It was almost like being on holiday.

One of Ebbutt's men had fetched his two suits from the cleaners. Everything else was unpacked. Now all he had to do was *think*—and it was surprising what little opportunity there had been for thought in the past twenty-four hours. He had to remember everything that had happened and everything he had been told, and try to make sense out of it—and also to plan what he should do.

Suddenly, he realised that so far he had done virtually nothing.

He remembered another case, on which he had been placed on the defensive from the very start, and had not recovered until it had been almost too late. From the beginning, Golden Boy had attacked—skilfully, viciously, unceasingly. Probably he would attack again and again.

In a way Grice had attacked him, too. So far, then, his mood had been almost entirely defensive, and that would not get him anywhere.

Attack would, but how could you attack the unknown?

He moved about the room unpacking, already feeling better; there must be a way, even if he couldn't as yet see it. Vague and almost nebulous thoughts ran through his mind, but that didn't matter, positive ones would come soon. It was nearly twelve-thirty—good lord, he hadn't even had breakfast! If he went down to the dining-room he would have to talk to a lot of other members, and be affable and pleasant to them——

Well, why *not*?

He went down, had a quick look at the smoking-room, which was almost empty, and then moved to the main bar.

He felt as if he had run into a brick wall, for there, at the bar, facing him, stood—Golden Boy.

It made no sense, of course; this was just a young man with gold-coloured hair and a fair complexion, he could have no possible connection with Golden Boy, but——

'Hallo, Rollison.' A member at the bar, standing with the youth, raised a hand. 'What's this I hear about you being dead?'

Rollison said mildly: 'People will exaggerate so.'

The youth laughed; an infectious chuckle.

'It certainly looks that way,' he said.

'Where did you hear it?' Rollison asked.

'A chap in the Bank,' answered the member. 'And there was something about an attempt to set fire to your flat, mentioned on the radio.'

'More or less the reason I'm here,' Rollison said.

'Dark deeds, eh?' said the member. 'Good lord—you don't know Johnny McAdoo, do you? Johnny—Richard Rollison. Hope your man wasn't too badly hurt, Rollison. What will you have?'

Rollison had a whisky and soda, as the member chatted on:

'Johnny's in the new production at the Westminster Theatre ... The hero, believe it or not ... Damn good part.' McAdoo made the normal disclaimer, admitted under questioning that he had a long part and the notices had been quite good. Then others came in and Rollison escaped to the dining-room, his head ringing with ideas. He had a corner table for one and could survey the whole room. At the far end, beyond a mass of tables and red leather chairs, were busts of old, celebrated members. On the walls were some fine oil paintings, flanked by two huge fireplaces as austerely cut as altars. Rollison, oblivious of these things, ate and considered. He had almost made up his mind when an older member paused in passing.

'When's the funeral, Rollison?'

Rollison watched him, thoughtfully, as he moved on, laughing, and out of the corner of his eye caught sight of a youth who came in, wearing one of the club's half-length waiter's jackets. The youth had long, dark, over-greased hair. Several other young waiters wore their hair long, too, there was nothing remarkable in it. But this one paused and looked round.

Then he saw Rollison.

His gaze rested on him for a fraction of a second, then passed on.

Rollison's heart began to beat faster.

Old Robinson, who looked like a film butler but had been deputy head waiter at the Carilon Club for many years, approached and spoke to the youth, then nodded as if satisfied. Rollison bent forward to scoop a piece of Stilton out of a round cheese.

The youth stood in the doorway.

Rollison tensed himself, but did not appear to be interested.

Quite deliberately the youth took his right hand from his pocket and pointed at the Toff.

Rollison flung himself to one side, and on the instant there was the crack of a shot. As he fell he heard shouts of: *'What's that?'* and then, unable to save himself, his head hit the corner of a chair. The blow stunned but did not knock him out. He was aware of the rush towards the door, and two words made a refrain in his mind: *'Stop him, stop him.'* A voice gasped: 'Blood!'

Blood?

He must have cut his head, of course.

'Give him air,' someone said.

'Stand back,' ordered someone else.

'Who is it?' demanded a third.

'Rollison,' someone answered, and the first speaker protested:

'But I thought he was dead.'

'*Dead!*' a man echoed in a tone of horror.

'Do you hear that?' demanded yet another. 'Rollison's dead.'

Dead, dead, dead, dead.

They thought him dead.

Then, a man knelt beside him. Close to him loomed the face of Dr. Webber, an old friend as well as a club member, and Rollison glimpsed the concern on the fleshy face. Webber was feeling his wrist and in a moment would know that his pulse was beating steadily.

Rollison whispered: 'I'm foxing, Webby.'

Webber started but didn't look up.

'Don't give me away,' breathed Rollison urgently.

Webber caught and found his wrist, felt for the pulse with a rather hot finger, held it, and then said:

'Let's have a stretcher.'

'Stretcher—*stretcher*!' a man roared.

It was strange to lie there, aware of the gaze of so many club members, the curiosity, the sense of shock, almost of horror. He heard the word 'murder' repeated several times. *Murder, murder, murder.* In a surprisingly short time he was being lifted on to a stretcher, carefully and expertly, and then carried out. Webber was by his side.

'Into the Number 2 dressing-room,' someone said with admirable presence of mind, and a door was opened and he was put on a bed against the wall.

'Leave him with me,' Webber said. 'I'll send when I want an ambulance ... On second thoughts, better have one along now,' he added. 'See to it, Phillips, will you?'

The man who had said: 'Into the Number 2 dressing-room,' said: 'I will, sir,' and a moment later the door closed.

'*Now* perhaps you'll tell me what all this is about,' Webber said in a quiet voice. 'Anyone would think you wanted to play dead.'

'That's *exactly* what I do want,' said Rollison. 'And I don't know whom I'd rather have to help me. And first, get me to a nursing home—not to a hospital.'

CHAPTER NINE

'DEAD AND ALIVE'

THE long-haired youth who had brazened his way into the Carilon Club slid out of a side door, now wearing the uniform of a delivery service, and made a rush towards a motor-cycle parked nearby. He saw police cars at the front of the hotel, and heard an ambulance, but so far there was no cordon, and no one attempted to stop him. He drove at a fair speed through the heart of London, moderately certain that he hadn't been followed. At Blackfriars Bridge he found a place to park, and walked briskly towards an empty telephone kiosk.

He dialled; and almost at once a honeyed voice answered: 'This is Goldy.'

'I've fixed him, Goldy,' the long-haired youth said.

There was a short pause before the voice spoke again, its tone overlaid with menace:

'You wouldn't have made another mistake, would you?'

'I tell you I've fixed him, Goldy.'

'When I go to the funeral,' said the Golden Boy, 'I'll believe it. And when I come away from the funeral you'll get your thousand pounds.'

'I can feel it in my pocket now,' said the long-haired youth.

'I hope you can. Okay, you know what to do. Get your hair cut——' He smothered a laugh which held a note of exultation, and went on: 'Then wait until I send for you.'

'Okay, Goldy.'

'And Mick.'

'Yes, Goldy?'

'Nice work.'

Mick's voice rose, like a child's: 'Thanks, Goldy! I told you I wouldn't let you down.'

The line went dead.

The youth stepped out of the kiosk and noticed two men hovering nearby. But men often hovered near telephone kiosks, there was nothing unusual in that. He sauntered towards the kerb—and for the first time felt a stab of alarm, for the men were closing in on him. One of them gripped his arm painfully.

'Here, what's your game?' Mick demanded. They weren't cops, they were too small for cops, that much was obvious. 'Let me go.'

The man gripping him said: 'You're coming with us ...'

'Or going straight to the police,' put in the other.

'I—I haven't done——'

The man gripping his arm said: 'Take his gun.'

The other man slid a hand into Mick's pocket, took out the gun, and slid it into his own. Mick's lips went dry. Walking abreast, they went to the station approach, and almost at once a taxi—its flag down—drew up.

'Inside,' one man said.

Mick put a foot inside, then spun round, pulled his arm free, and tried to run. The first man grabbed his arm and twisted savagely; Mick gasped. Between them, they pushed him into the taxi. The driver had seen what was happening, but took no notice. Passers-by appeared to see nothing. The taxi started up, and they went through the city, then pulled up near a telephone kiosk. One of the two men got out, and dialled the Blue Dog.

Bill Ebbutt answered with a wheezy: 'Who's that?'

The man said: 'It's Tiny. We got him.'

'Nice work, Tiny,' Ebbutt approved. 'Take him to Danny's place, everything's laid on.'

'Okay.' There was a pause before Tiny asked: 'Any news about the Toff?'

Drawing a deep breath, Ebbutt said: 'It looks as if they've got him this time.'

'My *Gawd*!' breathed Tiny.

The news first came over the B.B.C. at two-thirty.

'Mr. Richard Rollison, well known as a criminologist and perhaps better known as the Toff, died in a London nursing home today after a shooting affray in a West End club. It is understood that the man who fired the fatal bullet got away. An intensive police search is already taking place.'

And with this news, consternation spread.

It spread through the East End as well as Mayfair. It reached the shop in Chelsea where Jill Slater lost every vestige of colour and Jack stood behind the counter, looking as if he were made of stone.

It reached Rollison's relatives and friends.

It reached the hospital where Jolly lay . . .

Dr. Webber went there, ostensibly to see how Jolly was getting on. Jolly was in fact looking wan and lying flat on his back. When he saw and recognised Webber he tried to sit up, obviously in great alarm.

'Nothing to worry about,' Webber said. 'I came to tell you that you may read a certain fact concerning Mr. Rollison in the newspapers. Don't believe it. You have my word that it's not true, but that Mr. Rollison wants people to think it is.'

Jolly stared . . . and then gave a slow, quite happy smile.

'If they think he's dead they won't try to find and attack him, sir, will they?'

Webber chuckled.

But no one else was warned; at that stage only Jolly, Webber, a discreet sister at the private nursing home, and the Toff himself knew the truth. The headlines screamed:

TOFF DEAD

TOFF MURDERED

TOFF DIES IN CLUB SHOOTING

These and others in great variety were hurtled round the world. There were television shots of Rollison walking, of his Trophy Wall, of him discussing a case with Jolly. The obituaries ranged from the sensational in the *Mirror* to the discreet in *The Times*, but all told of his fifty triumphs and his cool, cold, courage.

The most touching of all, perhaps, was a brief interview with Grice, which appeared in every newspaper. In it, Grice stated:

> Richard Rollison was a very great detective. Hardly a professional living could not have learned something from him. Without the powerful organisation of a police force behind him, he achieved results which sometimes were little short of miracles. I shall miss him deeply.

Rollison read this in the *Daily Telegraph*, and recalled everything Grice had said to him. At least the Yard man would not feel he had neglected his duty; no one could have tried more. Sooner or later Grice must be told the truth, of course—but only Grice, and in such a way that no one else at the Yard had any reason to suspect the veracity of the reported death.

Rollison, in a small room at the nursing home, had the name *Wardle* on the door. His face was bandaged too completely for recognition, one eye being entirely hidden under a patch. The sister who was in the secret was not yet on duty, but by his side was a make-up box with everything he needed. He went to a plain whitewood dressing-table and began to make up very, very carefully what little showed of his face. He had almost finished when there was a tap at the door. His heart missed a beat, and then he told himself there was no need to fear anyone here.

'Who is it?' he called.

'Sister Mattison.' He recognised the voice.

'Come in, Sister.' Rollison turned round as the door opened. The sister, a small, compact woman, came halfway in and then stopped abruptly.

'Who——' she began, and then threw up her hands and

laughed. She closed the door, and then said with the laughter still in her voice: 'I would never have recognised you!'

'That's what I hoped,' said Rollison. 'Have you any news?'

'Yes, Dr. Webber telephoned. He has a room for you as Mr. Wardle at the Docks Hotel, Wapping. It's very small but clean, he assures me. And I've a suitcase and everything you asked me to get.'

'You're very good,' said Rollison.

'I'm glad to help,' she said. 'And I only hope you catch these criminals, and that those headlines'—she pointed— 'never come true.'

They stood silently for a moment, and then she moved back and asked in a more carefree voice:

'Is there anything more you would like me to do?'

'No,' said Rollison. 'Except—if I need to send any messages, may I call you as Wardle, and ask you to pass them on?'

'Of course,' she said. 'At any time.'

Twenty minutes later, carrying the suitcase, he walked out of the nursing home. His stride was shorter than usual and he needed time to perfect it. His shoulders were hunched, which took away a little from his height. He was in Bayswater, and turned a corner to a short parade of shops, one of them a newspaper shop. Three out of four posters and five out of six headlines on the rack outside were about him—and his photograph stared up from each front page. He took a taxi to Kings Road, Chelsea, near the Town Hall, then walked to the Slaters' shop. A woman and a child were coming out as he reached it, an old man was inside, talking to Jill.

He noticed at once that Jill looked more than distressed.

Her eyes were deeply shadowed, with the glassy stare that denoted sleeplessness. As Rollison stepped in, Jack Slater appeared from the back of the shop, tight-lipped and on edge. He glared at Rollison with hostility.

'Yes?'

Rollison was tempted to speak in his natural voice, and to

say: 'That's not the way to win business.' Instead, he asked for twenty Players and a book of matches, in tones pitched several degrees higher than normal.

The old man was saying: '... terrible, absolutely terrible! And he was as alive as I am only the other day. I was in the shop, I see him with my own eyes.'

Jill spun round and ran through the rear door, stifling her sobs.

Jack Slater growled: 'She's upset.'

'Has anything happened?' inquired Rollison.

Slater looked at him squarely. 'Yes, something's happened.' He paused, and Rollison waited almost breathlessly for the flash of recognition, it seemed impossible for Slater to be deceived at such close quarters. 'One of the few *decent* men left in England has been murdered—that's what's happened.'

'This—this Mr. *Roll*ison?'

'That's right.' The moment of testing was over, and Slater took the cigarettes and matches off the shelf.

Rollison handed over a ten shilling note.

'Was he a friend of yours, then?'

'You can say he was a friend,' Slater said.

The old man went out, muttering: 'I didn't mean to upset her.' Rollison went towards the door, but before it closed on him Slater had already gone in to comfort his wife.

Rollison went out, deeply moved—and very thoughtful. If two people who hardly knew him were so affected, how did those who knew him well feel? Ebbutt, for instance; Grice; Old Glory——

He stepped into a telephone kiosk and called a Mayfair number, and a woman answered briskly: 'Marigold Club.'

'Lady Gloria Hurst, please.' He used the assumed voice.

'I'm afraid Lady Gloria isn't available,' the woman said. Rollison recognised her voice, knew that he could almost certainly trust her—and yet dared not.

'It's extremely urgent and personal,' he said. 'I have a message from Mr. Jolly.'

'Mr. *Who*?'

'Jolly. J-O-L——'

'Hold on a moment,' the woman said, and Rollison waited for perhaps two minutes before his favourite aunt came on the line. She had a deep, resonant voice: she was a most remarkable woman and the only one of his relatives whom Rollison truly liked and respected.

'Who is that, please?'

'Is that Lady Gloria Hurst?'

'Yes.'

'Can we speak in confidence, please?'

'If you mean are we being overheard, *no*,' said Lady Gloria; and Rollison detected a sharp noise, and was quite sure that until that moment the operator had been listening-in. 'Now, what is this message about, Jolly?'

Very quietly, and in his natural voice, Rollison said: 'Don't believe all you hear in the next few days. Much of it isn't true.'

There was a hush; absolute and complete; and it lasted so long that Rollison wondered whether she could possibly have been cut off. Then he heard her speak; and he heard more—the huskiness in her voice, the stifled sob.

'Richard,' she said. 'Richard, don't ever do such a thing again. I really thought——' she broke off.

'I'm sorry, Glory,' Rollison said. 'It was a snap decision, and no one knows—except Jolly. Bless you,' he added softly.

In a stronger voice, she said: 'I thought that as it happened in the Carilon Club it really was gospel.' Her voice sharpened. 'Are you hurt?'

'No.'

'How long are you going to keep up this charade?' she demanded.

'Only a few days, I hope.'

'Is there anything you need?'

'Glory,' he said, 'let the world see that you're mourning for me.'

'I will,' she said, and then quite gently: 'Be careful, Richard.'

'I'll be very careful,' he promised, and rang off.

He stepped out of the kiosk and glanced up and down. A police car was on the other side of the road, and he recognised Chief Inspector Jackson, who glanced across and then looked away from him. Rollison walked along to a bus stop, stood with half-a-dozen other people, and took a No. 11 bus. He could go to Liverpool Street station on that, and go across to Wapping on another route. He climbed the curving staircase and found a seat at the front. He slid into it and watched the changing scene of London, the unceasing movement, the taxis and cars weaving about like giant ants among the pigmy people. Little people. 'Little' in the sense of obscure and anonymous people who did their daily job, mostly well, and asked for nothing more than enough to live on in comparative comfort.

Little people—like Martha and Joshua Penryn, like Jack and Jill Slater; like the customers and the shopkeepers throughout London. What was there about them that he liked? Why did he warm to them? Why did their fate matter to him so deeply?

Gradually, these thoughts changed. Swinging round Trafalgar Square, seeing the dense jungle of pigeons on the grey flag-stones, the photographers, the children thrilled and yet half-scared as pigeons pecked food from their hands or perched on their shoulders or their heads, the fountains playing and the bronze lions couchant at the foot of Nelson's Column, he wondered what he should do first.

The world believed him dead.

Webber would stall with the death certificate for a few days; but no more than a few days: he hadn't much time.

Golden Boy would be sure he was dead.

How *could* he attack Golden Boy?

CHAPTER TEN

VOICE FROM THE 'DEAD'

What I have to do, thought Rollison, is get him out of his hiding place. And he'll only come out if I've something he wants. I don't have anything he wants—as far as I know—and yet...

The ideas would not come.

He got off the bus at Liverpool Street station and heard a newsboy call out in a hoarse voice: 'Toff murdered—special.' He walked along Shoreditch towards Whitechapel, past the tiny warehouses and the factories where the little people sweated and worked, needles plying, machines whirring, to make dresses and lingerie, shorts and underwear. He passed the windows filled with buttons and bows, tapes and ribbons, passed cafés patronised by an endless flow of people, still without the idea he knew was lurking somewhere in the back of his mind.

He caught another bus, to Wapping High Street, then walked for a few minutes until he came to the Dock Hotel.

It was one of the riverside pubs which had retained its original character. Here a few rooms were available, usually to sailors who wanted to get away from their ship for a day or two, from the smells and the noises, the narrow companionways and the clank of steel boards. He knew Mrs. Battersby, the landlord's wife—not well, but well enough to be greeted as an old friend.

A short, metallic blonde with heavily made-up cheeks and glistening red lips, she looked at him without a sign of recognition.

'I'm Mr. Wardle,' Rollison said.

'Oh, *Wardle*,' she said in a voice as brassy as her hair. 'Booked by 'phone, didn't you?'

'That's right,' Rollison said. 'I was promised a room overlooking the river.'

'Only got one,' she said. 'Follow me.'

The staircase, of polished wood, was a semi-spiral, and the ceilings were low, but there was an air of old-worldliness here; of age. It had been a smugglers' haunt, and at times was a haven for smugglers to this day. Several doors led off a narrow passage, and Mrs. Battersby opened one on the right, and stood aside to let him pass.

Involuntarily, he exclaimed: 'But it's charming!'

'That's what all the guests say,' said Mrs. Battersby, and her voice was touched with pride. 'Bathroom's along to the left. No rules or regulations but if you make too much noise we'll throw you out.' She gave a harsh but not unfriendly laugh, and went out.

She had not asked a single question; his business was his own, and that was how it would remain.

The ceiling was oak beamed, the walls plain, off-white in colour, with a water-side etching here and there. The one window was gabled, he had to go close to it in order to see out, and what he saw was the wide expanse of London's river, with the docks and wharves on the other side, tall, new buildings in the distance, two ships sailing up-river. Only a hundred yards separated them—one from Bordeaux which would be heavy with wines, one from Copenhagen, probably loaded with butter and bacon, with ham and with cheese.

He heard a high, tinny tune, and a small pleasure boat crowded with sightseers came into sight, its loudspeaker blaring. It was a tape-recorder playing, of course, and badly amplified. He watched the boat pass, and then turned to unpack his few oddments.

It was now a little after three o'clock, and he was getting hungry.

It was after three o'clock, and he hadn't thought——

A *tape*-recorder.

Supposing he used a *tape*-recorder to fool Golden Boy.

He stood utterly still in the middle of the room, staring through the crooked window towards the shimmering water. He had known such moments before, when he knew that the 'flash' he needed was coming, when an idea was being born.

Golden Boy would come into the open *only* if he were driven or lured. What would lure him? No great prize, as far as Rollison could judge, but—fear? Fear that his identity might be revealed if he didn't.

Rollison was groping, as through a mist.

If Golden Boy believed there was a tape in existence which could lead to his identification and arrest, wouldn't he come out to get it? Or to *try* to get it?

He would have to.

The tinny tune faded into the distance.

Rollison pulled up a chair to the dressing-table and began to write. Soon, he was utterly absorbed in what he was doing . . .

And when it was done he believed he had found the answer, but he needed help. He needed help from Grice and from Ebbutt.

He had to be *very* careful.

And he had to remember that he hadn't much time.

Ebbutt's gymnasium was never busy during the day; a few men who worked by night might be there but it was not until evening that the place became full. Rollison stepped inside it, a little after four o'clock. A little wizened man was testing the ropes at the two rings, another was polishing a punch bag. Over in the far corner, the door of a tiny office was open and Rollison could see one of Ebbutt's legs.

The wizened man came up; a man Rollison had never really liked.

'Who'd you want?'

'Mr Ebbutt, please.'

'What about?'

'Insurance,' Rollison said.

The little man, who knew him well, did not move but said clearly:

'No callers except by arrangement.'

'Tell Mr. Ebbutt I am here, please.'

The man, who would normally have been falling over himself to oblige the Toff, was truculent and almost rude.

'You'll only be wasting your time—*and* his, and that's more important.'

'You might be costing Mr Ebbutt a great deal of money,' Rollison said more sharply.

'Listen, he won't see no one in the afternoon without an appointment. Now get out before I throw you out!'

Certainly Ebbutt did like his afternoons free; and certainly he, Rollison, was unaware of the normal way strangers were treated here. Would Bill Ebbutt himself behave like this?

He saw Ebbutt's legs move. Slowly, the man's huge body appeared, too large for the doorway; he had to squeeze through sideways. And on that instant, Rollison saw him as any stranger might: big, gross, bleary-eyed, with three chins and a veiny, broken nose—an ugly ex-prize fighter whose barrel-like torso was covered by a loose-fitting blue sweater, and whose trousers—despite his size—were too large for him. He wore torn canvas shoes which had once been white.

'What's up, Tack?' he asked the wizened man.

'I told this guy you don't see no one after lunch.'

'That's right, I don't,' Ebbutt said. He looked straight at Rollison and his gaze lingered. Rollison wondered whether there was a flicker of recognition in his eyes; wondered whether Ebbutt would be as ill-mannered as Tack. 'Unless it's urgent,' Ebbutt went on. 'Is this urgent, mister?'

'Very urgent indeed.'

'You'd better come in,' Ebbutt said, and stood aside.

Rollison entered the 'office', no more than a cubicle with a built-in desk, a high stool, and one wooden chair. The desk was littered with papers. Ebbutt stayed outside for a moment and there were sibilant whisperings. The wizened man's voice was raised at last in a kind of resigned protest.

'Okay, okay, if that's the way you want it.'

'Then don't forget it,' Ebbutt said. He pushed his way into the cubicle and went on gruffly: 'Okay, mister, what's so urgent?'

Rollison asked: 'Can that man hear us?'

'No. I've sent him away.'

Rollison moved and slid the door into position, then faced Ebbutt; only about four feet separated them. He smiled, and spoke very quietly in his normal voice.

'I never did like Tack much.'

Ebbutt went absolutely still. His face, until then tense and wary, seemed to have every expression smoothed out of it. He moistened his lips several times, tried to speak, and failed.

'I'm sorry, Bill,' Rollison said. 'This was the only way it could be. I don't think my Aunt Gloria will ever forgive me.'

Ebbutt drew in a great gulp of air, his body relaxed, he put both hands forward and took Rollison's; and very slowly, he said:

'Thank Gawd, Mr. Ar. Thank Gawd.'

Soon he was asking what the Toff was up to, and whether Grice wouldn't kick up a hell of a stink when *he* found out, and what could he, Ebbutt, do to help? This was about Golden Boy, of course, it had to be about Golden Boy.

'That's right,' said Rollison. 'I want to make him over-confident, Bill, and then I want to worry him. Now that he thinks I'm dead he might have a go at two or three raids tonight, to show the police he doesn't give a damn for them, either, so I'm going to ask Grice to make sure shops are very closely watched. Have your chaps keep a sharp look-out, too.'

'Every mother's son,' promised Ebbutt.

'And tell them to talk,' went on Rollison. 'Tell everyone to talk about the fact that I knew who Golden Boy was, and left a tape with all the information on it.'

'So?' Ebbutt's wheezing was growing in volume.

'No one knows where the tape is,' Rollison said. 'The police haven't got it. *You* haven't got it. Jolly might know where it is but he's in hospital and can't do anything about it. Following me, Bill?'

'Sure,' said Ebbutt, thoughtfully. 'Golden Boy starts to hunt for the tape.'

'That's right.'

'But he doesn't know where to look.'

'Yes,' said Rollison. 'First he worries. Then, he finds out.'

Ebbutt was smiling broadly. The bright periwinkle blue of his eyes outshining their less prepossessing qualities.

'How does he find out, Mr. Ar?'

'I don't know yet.'

'I think I can tell you,' said Ebbutt, in a tone of quiet triumph.

It was Rollison's turn to go still with surprise. He knew Ebbutt so well that he could not doubt that the ex-boxer had good news, and he could not imagine what that news could be.

'Out with it,' he said.

'The guy who shot at you in the club.'

'What about him?'

'He's a guest at Danny's,' Ebbutt said.

'He's a guest——' echoed Rollison, and he felt a great surge of excitement. 'You caught him, do you mean?' He could not imagine how, but Ebbutt's expression made it abundantly clear that he meant what he said.

'That's right, Mr. Ar,' said Ebbutt. 'Charley Dee and Tiny were watching you at the Carilon Club and when they heard what had happened they followed a suspicious looking guy who dashed out of the staff entrance. Picked him up at Blackfriars, and took him to Danny's place. Put him to sleep—he's asleep now, I'm to get a telephone call when he wakes up. Fact is,' went on Ebbutt heavily, 'I wanted to have a little talk with him before turning him over to Grice. Anonymous, I mean. I thought I might be more persuasive than the police. Don't you think so, Mr. Ar?'

Rollison said softly: 'If you can make him talk, we may not need anything else, Bill.' He was astounded at the news, astonished at the luck of it. 'And if he doesn't talk——'

'Or don't know enough,' put in Ebbutt.

'Or doesn't know enough,' agreed Rollison, 'we can leak a story about the tape.'

'Couldn't be better,' said Ebbutt with deep satisfaction. 'You going to have a go at him, or am I?'

'You,' said Rollison, 'and if you don't have any luck, I'll try.' He smothered a laugh. 'I can hardly believe——' he began, and broke off. 'I'd better see this chap before telling Grice I'm alive,' he went on. 'Until we've found Golden Boy, no one but you and Grice must know, Bill.'

'Cross my heart I won't even tell my wife,' promised Ebbutt solemnly. He gave a great bellow of laughter, cut it short in the middle, and peered anxiously towards the door as the telephone bell rang.

He plucked up the receiver.

'Ebbutt's Gymnasium,' he announced, then said with an ominous note in his voice: 'Okay, keep him that way.' He put down the receiver and nodded meaningfully. 'He's come round,' he announced. 'I can't wait to get my hands on him, Mr. Ar. If you *had* been dead, he'd have been your murderer.' After a pause, he added: 'We going together?'

'You go first,' said Rollison, 'and tell Danny you've arranged for me to go along. I don't want him wondering what I'm doing there.'

CHAPTER ELEVEN

DANNY'S PLACE

DANNY'S place was near the docks but not on the river front. It was not far from the main gates of the Millwall and East India docks, an old boarding house which had become a doss house years ago. Sailors without money, down-and-outs, and occasionally, men on the run from the police, stayed there.

It was used, occasionally, to hide individuals for several weeks at a time, and for this purpose there was a concealed attic, with only one small window in the roof. Traffic, mostly heading for the docks, passed noisily by, but no other sounds came in. The attic—like the whole place—was dirty and unsavoury. Rollison had been there only once or twice, but he knew it well by reputation. He was admitted by Danny, a bearded Swede, led to a loft ladder, and allowed to make his way up.

In the attic, cringing against a wall, was a small, long-haired youth—and Rollison had never seen one more frightened.

Opposite him was Bill Ebbutt.

Ebbutt was saying: 'You can have it your own way. Either you talk now, and don't get hurt, or you get hurt and talk later. Be sensible.' He glanced round at Rollison, grunted: 'So it's you,' and went on: 'Question Number One—what's your name?'

The youth gasped: 'Micky!'

'Micky what?'

'Micky—Moses.'

'That's a lie for a start.' Ebbutt doubled his fist, which looked like a great ham.

'It's not a lie!' gasped the prisoner. 'My name's Moses—my mother's name was Moses, I'm Michael Moses.'

'Who's Golden Boy?' demanded Ebbutt.

'I don't—I don't know what you mean!'

'Micky Moses,' Ebbutt said. 'You're going to get your nose broken.' He threw a mock punch, and the prisoner cowered back. 'Who is Golden Boy?'

'You—you mean Goldy!'

'I mean the boy with the golden hair who fixes these robberies.'

'That's—Goldy.'

'Goldy *who*?'

'I don't know. I swear I don't know.' Micky Moses turned a look of piteous entreaty towards Rollison, who had moved from the head of the ladder and was now squatting on a box. 'Make him believe me!'

'It's hard to believe,' Rollison said, in the assumed voice.

'It's the truth, it's God's truth!'

'Don't give me that,' growled Ebbutt. 'You killed Rollison on this guy's orders—but you don't know his name.'

'I don't, I swear I don't! Everybody knows him as Goldy.'

'Who is everyone?' demanded Rollison.

'The—the rest of us.'

'How many of you?'

'I don't know!' Micky Moses shot another glance of despairing appeal to Rollison. 'I've got a few pals, we—we go along with Goldy when he puts a job in our way. But we're not the only ones, Goldy—Goldy picks where he wants to.'

'So Goldy picks where he wants to,' Rollison said. 'What do you get out of it?'

'The—the dough.'

'What else?' demanded Ebbutt.

Micky Moses hesitated—and Ebbutt hit him savagely across the face.

The speed and power of the blow were astounding—it seemed impossible for so big and heavy a man to move so fast.

Micky went back against the wall, the back of his head thudded against it, his knees crumpled, and he nearly fell. Ebbutt made another swift movement, grabbed him by his collar, and hauled him to his feet.

'When I ask a question,' he said, 'I want an answer. *Quick.* What else do you get out of helping Goldy?'

Micky Moses gasped: 'A *shop*!'

Rollison heard the word clearly but did not immediately grasp its significance. Ebbutt stared at him, great fist raised, then pushed him further back against the wall, and growled:

'A shot of *what*?'

'Shop,' breathed Rollison, and then actually said aloud: 'Or did he *say* "shot"?'

'A—a *shop*!' cried Micky.

'Shop?' echoed Ebbutt, almost stupidly.

'My God,' Rollison whispered. 'A *shop*. You mean—one of the shops you've robbed?'

'Ye-ye-ye-yes!'

'What's this?' asked Ebbutt. 'All the takings from one robbery? That what you mean?'

'No!' cried Micky, almost in despair. '*I mean a shop—we get a shop—he gives us a shop!*'

Rollison said very slowly: 'The victim sells out, Golden Boy buys up the shop and gives it to you. Is *that* what you mean?'

'*Isn't it obvious?*' screeched Micky Moses.

'Not exactly obvious,' Rollison said more equably, 'but it's beginning to show through. Do you get a shop each?'

'No—among—among three or four.'

'So you are *given* a shop. You don't have to pay for it,' said Rollison very thoughtfully. He felt as he had when he had been searching for the idea; groping. 'Golden Boy——'

'*He's not Golden Boy, he's Goldy!*'

'Very well. Goldy,' corrected Rollison. 'He gives each group which helps him a shop—rent free?'

'No. We have to pay the rent, but we do that out of the takings.'

'I see,' said Rollison. 'The stock?'

'We get credit if we need it,' Micky Moses muttered. 'That's no problem.'

Rollison said: 'Who looks after the shops?'

'We do. Or our girl friends. There's always someone.'

'Yes. How much do you make out of it?'

Micky muttered: 'Anything up to fifty quid a week.'

'That means a turnover of six or seven hundred a week,' Rollison reasoned. 'Do they do as much business as that?'

'If they're run properly, they do.'

Rollison said doubtfully: 'Could be I suppose. So Goldy arranges with a group of you to take over a shop, after it's been robbed——' His mind boggled for a moment. The Slaters' shop might make that amount of money but old Penryn's probably hadn't taken more than a hundred pounds a week, possibly less. Did it average out? He wanted to ask a dozen questions but restrained himself. He asked two or three which convinced him that Micky Moses knew very little more than he had said. All appointments with Golden Boy were by telephone, and the telephones were always call boxes, as far as he knew. Golden Boy contacted groups of youths and gave them simple instructions, then set them up in business——

There must be more behind this than Micky Moses knew; no one would carry out such a campaign, with such daring, unless the stakes were high. Rollison hesitated. This might be the moment to finish with Micky, 'leak' the story of a tape-recorder message, and allow the youth to escape. He watched as Ebbutt glowered and Micky cringed—and he felt almost sorry for this boy who had set out to murder him in cold blood.

Ah!

'Moses,' Rollison said in a thin voice, 'why did you kill Mr. Rollison?'

It was a bizarre question to ask, and he saw Ebbutt glance

at him sharply; as if struck by a sudden doubt as to his identity.

The boy's answering voice was almost inaudible.

'Goldy made me.'

'So Goldy made you,' echoed Rollison softly. 'He ordered you to kill Mr. Rollison. Is that right?'

'Yes. Yes, I wouldn't have done it otherwise. He made me.'

'How many other men have you murdered?'

'None! I swear I haven't, I've never killed anyone before.'

'But you committed murder because *Goldy* ordered you to.'

'Yes. I've told you so, yes.'

'What's Goldy got on you?' asked Rollison, still more softly, but with menace in his manner. 'How is it Goldy can order you to commit murder, attack helpless people who have done you no wrong, and you obey him? Haven't you a mind of your own?'

'Yes. Yes, of course I have.'

'Ebbutt,' Rollison said, drawing back a few inches, 'we must learn what hold the man Goldy has over youths like Moses. And we haven't much time.'

Ebbutt made a swift movement with his clenched right fist.

'*No!*' screamed Micky Moses. 'Don't hit me again, don't hit me!'

'Then tell us what hold Goldy's got over you,' growled Ebbutt. 'Be quick about it, or I'll knock your head off your shoulders.'

'I'll tell you,' gasped Micky Moses. 'He'd stop our supplies, I couldn't live if I didn't have my supplies.'

In a cold voice, Rollison asked: 'Supplies of what?'

Micky Moses was almost whimpering and he looked at Rollison with a kind of piteous entreaty. Ebbutt dropped his hands to his sides and grunted:

'Should have known.'

'Yes,' Rollison said. 'The oldest and the newest cause. Drugs.'

'Drugs,' echoed Ebbutt.

They stood looking at the cringing youth with strange compassion, and as they did so, Micky Moses began to cry. It began as a whimper, and became a sob; and it reminded Rollison of the way Jill Slater had started to cry when she had realised how good her new neighbours had been.

He wondered what drug; but at the moment it did not greatly matter. He felt a great weight on his heart, a new burden. Youth and drugs. There was more trouble with youth than he could ever remember, a dissatisfaction, discontent, disquiet in them: and to some, drugs seemed the answer. In the short term it well might be, but it would rot the moral fibre, and in the end claim the life of every poor wretch who became an addict.

It was a long time since he had been directly involved in a drug investigation, and now he began to wonder whether Grice was aware of its nature, or whether he had been fooled.

Micky Moses was still crying.

'Turn off the waterworks,' Ebbutt growled, but there was a hint of sympathy in his voice.

'Have you got a supply now?' Rollison asked.

'Only—only for a day. Oh, God,' Micky gasped. 'Don't take it away, don't take it!'

'We won't take it,' Rollison said. 'One day you'll learn to give it up. Come on, Bill. Let's leave him.'

He went down the loft ladder first. Ebbutt followed, making the rungs creak. He lowered the hatch, but did not lock it. Reaching the narrow passage, Ebbutt said heavily:

'So now we know.'

'We know what the Toff was talking about, too,' Rollison said, and glanced up at the hatch; there was a small opening at one side where it hadn't latched. 'He must have known it was drugs.'

'He finds out,' Ebbutt said.

'If we could only get that tape,' said Rollison.

'Tape?' echoed Ebbutt.

'Don't you know about that?'

'I don't know a thing.'

'Rollison put everything he'd learned on a tape,' Rollison said, quite clearly. 'He told Grice he knew what the case was about and who was behind it, but he hadn't got the evidence yet. He said he had a presentiment about this case, he wasn't going to live through it, so he made a tape-recording of everything he knew.'

'And we don't know where the tape is?' cried Ebbutt.

'Keep your voice down!' Rollison said, as if in sharp rebuke.

In the attic, Micky Moses was crouching close to the hatch cover. He could hear clearly when no traffic was passing outside, but some of the words were drowned. Tears still smeared his cheeks, his face was drained of all colour, but there was a glitter in his eyes. He heard Ebbutt cry:

'And we don't know where the tape is!'

'Keep your voice down,' the other man ordered.

Micky Moses drew closer to the hatch, and hardly dared to breathe. A bus or lorry rumbled past and he waited until the sound died away. He heard the men below whispering, and now he lay flat on his stomach with his ear to the narrow opening.

'He must have told someone,' Ebbutt was saying.

'I think I know who he told,' the other man said.

'Was it Jolly?'

'No, it certainly wasn't Jolly,' the other answered.

'What will you do if you find it?'

'Take it to the police of course.' The man was quite decisive. 'This is too dangerous to play with, Ebbutt. If Rollison had sent it to the police himself, he'd be alive today.'

'I can't argue about that,' Ebbutt said.

'We'd better be going,' Micky heard the second man say. 'Did you shoot that bolt?'

'Of course I did,' said Ebbutt, indignantly.

Their footsteps slowly faded, while Micky Moses got to his feet, sweat dripping off his forehead. His lips were trembling, and he kept muttering to himself.

'I must get away—must tell Goldy—must get away ...'

He scrabbled at the hatch, and found that it was not quite closed.

CHAPTER TWELVE

ESCAPE

Downstairs at Danny's, Rollison said: 'Watch him, Bill.'

'Wherever he goes, I'll know,' Ebbutt promised.

'And I'll see Grice,' Rollison went on.

'If Grice's boys watch they might give themselves away,' said Ebbutt.

'Grice would love to hear you say that,' said Rollison drily.

'You know the risk,' Ebbutt said. 'But I daresay you're right. This isn't a job we can handle without telling the Yard. If it blew up in our faces we'd only have ourselves to blame. Okay, Mr. Ar. There's one thing.'

'Yes?'

'You've stuck your neck out again.'

'It does rather look as if that's its natural position.'

'It won't make any difference whether we bury you as Wardle or Rollison,' said Ebbutt with heavy humour.

Rollison said appeasingly: 'But there's no immediate danger, Bill. It can't start until Micky Moses has got through to Goldy. Take it easy!'

Ebbutt looked at him squarely, and said: 'Don't know what fear is, Mr. Ar, do you?'

Rollison gripped his arm, said: 'Don't I, Bill?' and turned away. Soon he was on a bus heading for Aldgate; and every brown-haired youth he passed seemed to be a potential victim of Golden Boy, and every fair-haired one his own potential murderer. He took a train at Aldgate East for Charing Cross, then walked along the busy Embankment towards the Yard. The tulips were nearly over, phlox and aster and antirrhinum were in the beds, a glory of colour. He went into the Yard, and although most of the policemen he saw knew him as Rollison, none seemed to recognise him. The sergeant on duty in the hall asked:

'Is Mr. Grice expecting you?'

'No. But tell him I've a message from Lady Gloria Hurst.'

The sergeant said: 'Okay, then.'

Soon, he was saying: 'Mr. Grice will send out for you. He won't keep you a minute.'

Rollison stood at the window by the big round reception table, looking out on the river. Almost at once a big, youthful-looking man came into the hall.

'Mr. Wardle?'

'Yes.'

'Mr. Grice can see you now, sir.' The big man was a stranger to Rollison.

Rollison walked with him along the familiar passage, stopped at the familiar door, and followed the other in.

'Mr. Wardle, sir,' he said.

Grice was standing behind the big desk on which were placed in neat precision an IN and OUT and PENDING tray. The door faced the window, and Rollison was acutely aware of the bright light and the detective's searching gaze. The door closed. Grice did not offer his hand, but motioned to the chair which Rollison normally hitched round. This time he simply sat down. Once again he wondered how an old friend would behave to a stranger; whether Grice had one manner for cronies, one for others.

'I understand you've a message from Lady Gloria Hurst.'

'That's right,' said Rollison in his Wardle voice.

'What is it?'

Rollison said: 'Apparently Mr. Rollison left a tape-recorded message for you and told her about it before his murder,' Rollison said. 'She didn't think it wise to tell you about it personally.'

'Why did she think it wise to tell *you* about it?' Grice asked.

Until that moment he had been civil enough, but aloof and impersonal; the Grice of many years ago. Now, something obviously startled him, and his manner changed. He sat absolutely still, with an almost predatory look.

'I am an old servant of Lady Gloria's,' Rollison went on, 'and she imposes great trust in me. I——'

Grice said in a thin, almost disillusioned voice: 'And I *believed* Webber.'

Rollison stopped speaking.

'Yes,' Grice said. 'I actually thought you were dead.' They eyed each other for a few moments and then he went on: 'You would have fooled me in a crowd. Who made you up?'

'All my own work,' Rollison said. 'We can't be overheard, can we?'

Grice said: 'I'll make sure.' He went to the passage door and locked it, lifted a telephone and said into it: 'I don't want to be disturbed by anyone about anything.' There was a faint echo of 'Very good, sir,' as he replaced the receiver. 'Why didn't you warn me in advance?' he demanded, and then went on: 'Another of your flashes of inspiration, I suppose.' He was obviously talking himself out of shock, and Rollison did not speak. 'Wild horses wouldn't have dragged out what I said about you if I hadn't been convinced you were dead. You'd better have a good reason for——'

He broke off.

'Being alive,' murmured Rollison.

They both laughed, on a low note, and Grice became much more himself, standing up and beginning to pace the office, glancing now out of the window, now at Rollison as if to make sure he was seeing straight.

'Why?' he demanded at last. 'Presumably you think you can help better if they think you're dead.'

'Yes,' said Rollison. 'Bill—do you know what Golden Boy is up to?'

'No,' Grice said. 'Do you?'

'Do you know that he buys up little shops and hands them

over to friends like my murderer?'

'*He* buys them!' gasped Grice. 'How did you find this out?'

Rollison told him all that had happened, leaving out only the part played by drugs. Grice made one or two notes but no comment until Rollison had finished. Then he said crisply:

'This isn't a job to leave to Ebbutt's men.'

'They caught Micky Moses,' Rollison pointed out.

'And everything they did after that was unlawful—they should have taken him to the nearest police station,' retorted Grice. He gave an unamused laugh. 'Alive or dead, you don't think much of the law, do you?' He picked up a telephone and said: 'Get me Mr. Hill, of Wapping Division.' He put the receiver down, and went on almost defiantly to Rollison: 'We'll have to pick Moses up at once, of course. You realise that, don't you?'

'Bill,' said Rollison. 'You and Bill Ebbutt can work together on this. Have Hill talk to Ebbutt and decide the best way to handle it. Don't pick Moses up—let him lead to Golden Boy. He's the only clue you have. Don't throw it away.'

'The moment you came and told me this it became official,' Grice said.

'No one else heard. No one but you is in command. You don't have to go by the book, Bill. I couldn't let you go on thinking I was dead, I couldn't tell you I was alive without explaining what it was all about. If you pick up Micky Moses you'll lose any chance of finding Golden Boy. Don't throw the chance away, Bill. You might do a lot of harm if you do.'

Grice said sharply: 'You're keeping something back.'

'Well, yes, I am.'

'What is it?'

'The motive for the whole business.'

'Are you sure?'

'I think I'm sure.'

'Then tell me,' Grice ordered.

'No,' said Rollison. 'If you're going to pick Micky Moses

up, I'm not going to tell you a thing more. If you work with
Ebbutt——'

He broke off, and in the pause which followed, the telephone rang. This would be Hill, of the Division. Grice let the
instrument ring and it seemed to go on for a long time. There
was a break in it—then it rang again. Grice lifted the receiver,
and said into it: 'Hold him on for a moment.' He held his
hand over the receiver, and went on: 'You think Golden Boy
will come after you, as Wardle.'

'I do.'

'What the devil makes you ready to take such chances?'
demanded Grice, almost angrily. 'It's sheer madness.' He put
the receiver to his lips. 'Put Mr. Hill through ... Hallo,
George ... The Rollison business and the shop crimes ... I'm
told Ebbutt of the Blue Dog has discovered something. Co-
operate with him, will you. It's a question of keeping tabs on
two or three men without them knowing they're being watched
... Yes, see Ebbutt as soon as you can ... Do you know much
about the Docks Hotel these days? ... I want the place
watched without the remotest possibility of it being suspected
... Is it possible? ... Yes, ask Thames Division to help,
probably they can keep an eye on it from the river ... I don't
know as much as I'd like to yet, but there's a man named
Wardle—WARDLE—who might be in danger and might be
able to help us. I'll call you again later tonight ... Thanks.'

Grice rang off.

'Well?' he said, demandingly.

'Golden boy *alias* Goldy blackmails his strong-arm men,'
said Rollison. 'He holds back their supplies of drugs.'

Grice echoed in an almost inaudible voice: *'Drugs?'*

Rollison nodded. It was fascinating to see the effect of this
on Grice; to find this hardened policeman shocked and shaken.
He waited long enough for Grice to say:

'Who told you?'

'Micky Moses.'

'Could he be lying?'

'Hardly. He appeared to have all the symptoms.'

After a pause, Grice said: 'It would explain a lot.' He gulped. 'It would explain the boldness of it, if they're hopped up when they raid the shops they wouldn't care what happened. And if they're addicts——' he broke off.

'Bill,' Rollison said, 'how many shops have changed hands after the raids?'

'Difficult to be sure,' Grice answered cautiously. 'But each could become——' he paused.

'A distribution centre for drugs,' Rollison put in.

'Yes. And a lot of other shops *could* be controlled by Golden Boy or whoever is behind him,' Grice said. 'Rolly, I've never liked the look of this case, not from the beginning. We've never——' he ran a hand over his chin, showing his feelings in a way rare in him. 'We've never had a major drug problem in London, but there are so many teenagers behaving badly that this *could* have spread a long way already. Do you know anything else at all?'

'No,' said Rollison. 'But I think I'll have a visitor, soon.'

'At the Docks?'

'Yes.'

'You could be attacked——'

'Oh, no,' said Rollison. 'Not while Golden Boy thinks I can put my hands on that tape. The first thing he'll try is to bribe me.' He gave a short, unamused laugh. 'I think I'll go and wait for him.'

Grice said: 'Don't take a chance you needn't, Rolly. And—thanks.'

'Forget it,' said Rollison. 'May I use your telephone? I'd like to talk to Ebbutt ... Thanks'. He lifted the receiver. Before long, the call came through. 'Hallo, Bill,' Rollison said. 'Any news?'

'Moses escaped an hour ago,' Ebbutt reported. 'He made a telephone call from a kiosk, and now he's waiting at a shop in Bethnal Green. A general tobacco and sweet shop,' Ebbutt added. 'I've got it closely watched.'

Rollison said: 'I'll call you from the Docks Hotel.'

He would have given a great deal to follow up Micky Moses, but his turn hadn't come, yet.

Micky Moses waited in the back of the shop, painfully on edge. He was ashen pale, as he monotonously rubbed one hand against the other, while moistening his lips. An elderly man was in charge of the shop; he had asked no questions, shown no curiosity.

A motor-cycle engine sounded, and a youth pulled up outside, helmeted, leather-jacketed, quick-moving. He put the machine on its stand, and approached briskly. Micky Moses drew back, acutely disappointed. This wasn't Goldy, and Goldy was late. If only he knew what threatened.

The back-room door opened and the motor-cyclist came through. Moses stared in surprise—and then with dawning recognition. The motor-cyclist locked the door, and then asked in a low-pitched voice:

'What's this all about, Micky?'

'Goldy!' cried Micky Moses. 'It couldn't be worse, it——'

'Keep your voice low and keep a hold on yourself,' said Goldy sharply. 'Just tell me what you know.'

Moses told him ... of the kidnapping, the attic prison, Ebbutt, the stranger named Wardle, the tape-recorder. He repeated the conversation between Ebbutt and Wardle almost word for word, while Goldy nodded from time to time. At last, Goldy said:

'How did you get away?'

'I managed to get the hatch open, it wasn't easy but I managed it.'

'Anyone follow you?' demanded Goldy.

'Of course they didn't—they didn't know I'd escaped.'

'I hope they didn't,' said Goldy. His voice was still honeyed but there was an edge to it. 'You go to the Lewisham shop and wait for me there. Don't go out—understand. Wait for me.'

'I'll wait, Goldy, don't you worry,' Moses muttered. 'I'll wait all night if I have to.'

Goldy left . . .

Fifteen minutes later, Micky Moses left, and two of Golden Boy's youths followed him. As far as they could judge, no one else did. When Golden Boy heard this he put down the receiver in a telephone kiosk near Whitechapel Church; paused; then called another number.

'I want to know everything there is to know about a place called the Docks Hotel, in Wapping. And I want to know who's staying there—especially any man on his own.'

He put down the receiver again.

CHAPTER THIRTEEN

VISITOR FOR THE TOFF

ROLLISON went in by the side door of the Docks Hotel. Not far along two women were walking briskly, one pushing a pram; in the other direction a man and a girl were standing close together and talking in the whispers of lovers. Opposite the front entrance a brewer's dray had parked, and not far behind it a van which Rollison had seen before—or at least, one very like it. It was dark blue with white lettering, and the wording on the side was TOBY'S—TOBACCO—CONFECTIONERY. Two or three small shops were opposite the hotel, but it was after six—late for wholesalers to deliver.

No one appeared to notice him go in.

He passed a prepayment telephone at the head of the stairs, then walked along to his own room. He took out his key, examining the lock almost by habit as he did so.

There were bright scratches on it.

He paused. He had not noticed the scratches before, but on that occasion Ma Battersby had opened it, and he had not taken particular notice. These scratches were very bright indeed—they must have been done in the last few hours or they would have dulled.

He took out a cigarette case and selected a cigarette—which was in fact a blow-pipe, one from the precious store which had not been damaged at his flat. Keeping it between his lips, he opened the door. Pushing it back slowly at first, he banged it suddenly against the wall, darting to one side.

At the far end of the room, back to the window, was a young woman.

The light was too poor for him to see her clearly, but she looked young. One hand was raised in front of her, as if his coming had taken her by surprise; the other was by her side. Both were empty.

She gave a little laugh.

'Are you nervous?' she asked.

She had a pleasant voice, a little too careful—but he liked the laughter which stayed in her words.

'Yes,' he said.

'There's no need to be nervous of me.'

'I'm always nervous of attractive young women who break into my room,' Rollison said drily. He had almost forgotten he was 'Wardle'. Had she noticed?

'Perhaps it doesn't happen often enough to you,' she said.

She had hardly moved, and was looking at him searchingly. The window let in what light there was, and it fell fully on to his face. He moved nearer her, and to one side; and as he had already started flippantly, he went on in the same strain:

'Is this visitation laid on by the hotel?'

'No,' answered the girl. 'It's a speciality exclusively for you.'

'What have I done to deserve it?' demanded Rollison.

He glanced round the room. There were only two places where anyone could be hiding—one under the double bed, one inside the big, old-fashioned wardrobe. She had no handbag; then he saw it on the dressing-table.

'It isn't what you've done, it's what you're going to do,' she said.

'So you have second sight,' remarked Rollison.

'Over this I have,' she said.

Rollison hesitated—then went even closer. She *was* young; nineteen or twenty, he guessed. She was a very dark brunette, heavily made-up—far too heavily for a girl of her age. Her linen suit was simple in cut and of dark green. Her eye-shadow was green, too.

Her smile hardly warmed, but her expression was set, as if she wondered what he was going to do.

'Turn round,' he ordered.

'Why should I——'

He shot out an arm and spun her round, pushing her away as he did so. While she was recovering her balance, he snatched a look under the bed, and by the time she had steadied, he had opened the wardrobe door.

'What did you do that for?' she demanded angrily.

'I wanted to find out whether you were alone.'

'Can't you see I am?'

'But I don't trust you,' Rollison said. 'Should I?'

She did not answer at once, but continued to glare at him, making no attempt to conceal her anger; a spoilt little brat beneath the charm, Rollison decided.

'Are you going to tell me what you want or am I going to have to force the truth out of you?' he demanded, going a step closer.

She shrugged her shoulders. 'It's quite simple. I'm here to tell you that if you play your cards sensibly you can pick up a thousand pounds.'

'Oh, can I,' said Rollison softly. 'How——'

He heard a faint sound behind him, and for the first time since seeing the girl, he felt acute alarm. He backed swiftly against a wall, and then saw the door slowly opening. He put the unlit cigarette to his lips again, his heart beating fast.

Three youths came in——

And behind them came Golden Boy.

The most frightening thing about their entry was its quietness and lack of fuss. Golden Boy closed the door behind him, almost soundlessly. Rollison, half-aware of the fact that both Ebbutt and the police were watching, of the fact that Golden Boy couldn't possibly escape, was far more concerned with the atmosphere of menace the four brought with them. He could understand the terror which they struck in such people as the Penryns and the Slaters.

And Golden Boy conveyed that menace far more acutely than the others.

The girl watched him. One long-haired youth stood by the

door, the two others ranged themselves on either side of Rollison. Golden Boy stood in front, only two yards away. The beautiful skin seemed without blemish, the clear eyes were neither hostile nor friendly: simply intent.

'What do you know about Rollison?' he demanded.

Rollison gulped. 'He—was murdered.'

'Take your cigarette out of your mouth when you speak to me,' said Golden Boy flatly. 'How well did you know him when he was alive?'

Slowly, Rollison took the cigarette out of his mouth. His thoughts raced, to find the kind of answer which would satisfy this young devil. He had come about the non-existent tape-recording of course, the answer must relate to that in some way.

'I worked for him,' he answered.

'Doing what?'

'Making—inquiries.'

'Inquiries about what?'

'Anything he wanted to know.'

'Such as?'

Rollison drew a deep breath, and said defiantly: 'You.' When Golden Boy did not prompt him, he went on: 'About you and what you're doing with the shops.'

'How much did you find out?'

Rollison muttered: 'There wasn't much time to find out anything. He wanted me to discover if the new owners of the shops were in any racket. He was after you, all right.'

'It's a good thing I got after him first,' said Golden Boy. The sneer in his voice was the nearest to emotion he had yet shown. 'How much did he find out?'

'I don't know.'

'How do I know you aren't lying?'

Rollison felt a sudden tightening of his muscles, but he did not reply at once. Golden Boy glanced at the two youths close to him, and they edged a little nearer; either could touch him by stretching out a hand. He wondered what they would do, or try to do, if they were ordered to attack him. Golden Boy did not move, and yet in a strange way he, too, seemed to be within touching distance.

'If you knew anything about Rollison, you'd know he was pretty secretive,' Rollison answered at last. 'He didn't take me into his confidence—he didn't take *anybody* into his confidence. I don't know a thing——' he moistened his lips and his glance rested for an instant on each of the youths, then passed on to the girl who seemed now to be amused by the interrogation. 'Except that he made a tape he said I would get if anything happened to him.'

'Something happened to him, all right,' said Golden Boy. 'Did you get the tape?'

'I haven't had it yet.'

'Expect to get it?'

'Oh, yes.'

'Tape from the dead?' sneered Golden Boy.

'He'd probably leave it at his bank and have them post it to me.' Rollison wiped his forehead, and gulped again. 'I don't know, I tell you——'

'Which bank?'

'He banked at MidPros, in Piccadilly.'

'So they have the tape.'

'I didn't say so!' gasped Rollison. 'I only said they might have.'

'You got any letter or anything to show the bank?'

'No! But he's sent messages to me before. I've worked for him for a long time but very few people knew it, he——'

'Where would he send it? Here?'

Why not here? Rollison wondered. It was as good a place as any. But how could Rollison have known he was to come here? Before long he would be asked that, be asked *why* he had come to the Docks Hotel. Unless he was very careful he would set a trap into which he would fall himself. He did not glance at the door, but measured the distance in his mind's eye. If he got out, the others would rush after him, the police and

Ebbutt's men would take them prisoner almost without a fight.

'*Answer my question!*' said Golden Boy softly. 'Or——'

Rollison put the cigarette to his lips, as if with nervous forgetfulness, then blew the tear gas phial inside it straight into Golden Boy's face. He saw a momentary flash of horror in those clear eyes, then Golden Boy backed away, gasping:

'Get him!'

The others moved, but for a split second they were distracted by the sharp sound of the breaking phial. It gave Rollison time to reach the youth nearest to him. He gripped his wrist and twisted, then flung him towards Golden Boy and the girl. The only threat to Rollison for the next moment was the guard at the door.

This youth had a knife in his hand, and crouched, ready to use it.

Rollison leapt at him, bodily. The knife caught in Rollison's jacket but he felt no pain. He hurtled into the youth, sending him back against the door with a sickening thud. All were now coughing as the tear gas caught their eyes and noses. Rollison pulled open the door—and saw two more youths, obviously startled, obviously tough. One of these, too, had a knife.

Rollison did the only possible thing: he raced along the passage, flinging his arms out, catching one youth and sending him staggering, knowing any second that the knife might plunge into his back. The short passage seemed to grow longer with every step.

Rollison reached the head of the stairs.

Then he felt a searing pain in his left arm—and knew that the knife had stabbed into him. He staggered, but regained his balance. He grabbed the handrail and almost fell down the stairs, heard another shout behind him, half-expected another knife, or a bullet—anything.

The side door was straight ahead—closed.

He reached it and flung it open. Here was safety, the police and Ebbutt's men would make sure of that. He turned towards

Wapping High Street—and again he missed a step.

At least a dozen youths were in sight. A *dozen*.

All were staring at him.

Rollison could see through gaps in the buildings on one side—and was appalled. The High Street was crammed with long-haired youths, who were gathered in little groups or patrolling up and down. There was no sign of police or Ebbutt's men, who must have been so heavily outnumbered that they had no chance at all.

Nor had Rollison, if he went that way.

He turned towards the river and the steps leading down to it; the Thames Division would have it covered, that was his way of escape. But again he pulled up short, this time in horror.

The river was swarming with small craft.

There were rowing boats, launches, and small motor-boats, all of them manned by long-haired youths, all turning towards the foot of the steps, and at the same time the side door burst open again.

Golden Boy, tears streaming down his face, came out.

CHAPTER FOURTEEN

THE MOB

ROLLISON saw the youths behind Golden Boy pause, knew that there was no possibility of escape and none of rescue. In that moment he did not think he had any chance at all, and his blood seemed to turn to ice.

Then he saw what might be a chance.

Golden Boy——

The boy was shading his eyes and staring towards him, wiping tears away with one hand. Whether he saw Rollison or not was doubtful, but no one could doubt the rage in him. Rollison, trapped, put another 'cigarette' to his lips, turned, and hurried towards him, his left arm painful but not bad enough to handicap him. As they drew closer, Golden Boy seemed to recognise him, and he dropped his hand from his eyes to his pocket.

Rollison blew the phial.

Golden Boy, either half-blinded by the previous phial or by his rage, did not appear to see it coming, and it struck him just beneath his nose; perfect. As it did so he half-dragged a pistol from his pocket, but the tear gas stung and he let the gun slide back, gasped, and clapped his hands to his face.

Just behind him, coming from the road, were three youths.

Just behind Rollison, no more than ten yards away, were two youths from the river.

And from the side door of the Docks Hotel, two more youths came.

Rollison reached Golden Boy, gripped his arm, and thrust it upwards behind his back, said: 'Do as you're told or I'll break your arm,' and at the same moment slid his left hand into the other's pocket. The stab wound in his own arm hurt, he

flinched but did not slow down. He touched the gun. Beyond
Golden Boy he saw the youths, uncertain what to do. He
twisted round so that his back was against a wall and he could
not be attacked from behind. He thrust Golden Boy's arm up
further—in a moment it would crack. The boy was holding his
breath with pain.

Rollison pointed the gun upwards, and pulled the trigger.
The crack of the shot sounded deafening in the narrow alley,
and he saw the youths flinch.

He said: 'I'll shoot you through the heart if you play any
tricks.' He raised his voice: 'Hear that? I'll kill him if you
don't make a path for me. *Hear that*, Goldy. Tell them to clear
a path!'

Golden Boy gasped: 'Let him—go.'

'Not me—*us*,' Rollison said.

He kept tight hold of the gun with one hand and of Golden
Boy with the other, but his own wound was now throbbing,
and he would not be able to keep this up for long.

'*Run!*' he urged, and pushed Golden Boy forward.

They approached the High Street at a shambling trot, and
the long-haired youths in the alley pressed back against the
wall to let them pass. As they reached the street, Rollison
looked up and down in almost stupefied amazement.

The wide street between high warehouse walls was packed
with youths.

They were gathered together in a loose mob stretching as far
as the eye could see. Some were dark and some were fair, some
were tall and some were short—but in a strange way, they all
seemed the same. They wore dozens of different colours, and
varieties of shirts and tunics, suits and jeans—and yet all
seemed identical.

Every face was turned towards the Toff and Golden Boy.

Rollison glanced up—and at the windows of the warehouses,
even on the tall roofs, he saw more long-haired youths. No one
else was in sight, police and Ebbutt's men and passers-by had
been driven out of the street by this solid phalanx of staring

youths between the ages of sixteen and twenty.

Rollison said in a taut voice:

'Tell them to let us through.'

Golden Boy said: 'You're not going through, now or at any time.'

'Tell them, or I'll break your arm!'

Golden Boy said in a vicious voice: 'Break my arm then. If you do, they'll tear you to pieces.'

He meant it. Whatever else, he had rare physical courage, and he showed it now in such a way that all who were close to him must be aware of it. That sea of faces, that press of bodies, was close and threatening, and unless he could frighten this boy into giving an order, then soon—*very* soon—he would be dead, for they would tear him to pieces.

There were savage faces, sullen faces, vicious faces, and all were staring at him. It was like a nightmare; and it was worse than a nightmare because of the pain of the knife wound and the fear that Golden Boy created, a fear beyond Rollison's imagining or experience.

All these things passed through his mind in seconds, while he stood on the pavement, aware of those eyes and faces behind him and above him as well as on all sides.

'Goldy,' he said tensely, 'I mean what I say.'

'And *I* mean what I say.' On the instant Golden Boy raised his voice, and that made Rollison aware of a sharp, uncanny thing. Until that moment there had been silence; no scuffling of feet, no talking, no shouting: just silence. Above this silence Golden Boy's voice sounded with unbelievable clarity —almost as if he were singing with the purity of a choir-boy before his voice had broken.

'If he breaks my arm, tear him to pieces!'

There was a kind of sigh for an answer, as if they had heard, and were telling him that they would do what he told them.

'That's enough,' he said to Rollison. 'Let me go.'

There was no answer.

'I won't warn you again,' said Golden Boy. 'Let me go.'

There was nothing, absolutely nothing, that Rollison could do except break this devil's arm—and then feel the sudden rush of savage slaves converging on him in maniacal attack. He knew he had no choice; he could not sway this multitude from any purpose to which Golden Boy set his mind. He had never felt so utterly helpless in his whole life.

Then he heard a curious whistling sound—and glanced up. He saw what seemed like a rocket hurtling towards him from one of the loading bays of a warehouse. Beyond were men—men pointing guns. The 'rocket' struck the wall just above his head, and burst. Vapour filled the air, reaching his nose, his throat, with a hot, suffocating impact. He felt himself sagging away from Golden Boy, hazily aware that he, too, was choking.

All, now, began to retch and cough, as other 'rockets' burst, against walls, on the roadway, on heads and shoulders, until the whole street was a seething mass of struggling, screaming, youths. Rollison found himself pushed back, back, down the way he had come, until he was finally crushed against the door of the Docks Hotel.

Almost unconscious, he felt his knees bending, his legs giving way, when the door behind him opened, and he was pulled inside.

The door closed, and a miraculous quiet fell about him. Coolness touched his face; and he heard voices—one of them familiar.

'How is he?' That was Grice.

'He'll be all right, sir.'

'Get him to a bedroom.'

'He can't walk——'

'Then carry him!' snapped Grice.

In the half-world of pain and fear that enclosed him, another fear caught Rollison. He thought *mind my arm, mind my arm*. He was lifted gently by two men, one at the ankles, one at his shoulders. He almost screamed *mind my arm* but no sound came. He felt his body being effortlessly moved as they

started up the stairs. Then, agonisingly, his arm touched a
banister post and he felt pain shoot through his whole body.

'Careful with him.'

'What's the matter with his arm?'

'It's bleeding, see.'

'Careful.'

'What's that about blood?' Grice demanded.

'Some trouble with his left arm, sir.'

'Have a look at it as soon as you can,' Grice ordered.

Sounds came from outside—the high-pitched wailing of an
ambulance siren, other sirens, whistles—a distorted voice.
Rollison remembered the clarity of Golden Boy's voice when
he called out, this was something quite different, harsh,
garbled, a scrambled voice. Someone speaking over a loudspeaker, of course, giving orders to the youths.

Orders—youths—orders—youths—Golden   Boy—golden
voice.

Mind my arm!

'Did you say something, sir?' a man asked.

'In there,' called someone else.

'Mind my arm, please!'

'We'll look after it, sir.'

Then there was quiet, disturbed only by breathing and
shuffling sounds. He was in a room and the door had closed.
He was laid very gently on a bed, and then felt hands at his
shoes—felt them being slipped off, felt hands at his jacket.
They helped him to sit up and took the jacket off his shoulders
carefully, drawing the sleeve from his injured arm with even
greater care. The sleeve came inside out—and the pale-
coloured lining was soaked with blood. One man unfastened
his shirt-sleeve and began to roll it up.

'Scissors,' said another.

'Scissors.'

'Scissors!'

A pair of blunt-tipped scissors appeared in one man's hand.

'We'll have to cut the sleeve, Mr. Wardle.'

Rollison nodded, and thought: so they still know me as Wardle. Grice didn't, anyhow. Rollison tried to think of what was going on outside but could not really keep his mind off the arm. A man was washing it, cautiously; funny how gentle big, clumsy-looking men could be. The door opened and a voice asked:

'Superintendent Grice here?'

'He just went out. Who wants him?'

'The streets are clear,' a man said. 'And the Press is out there in strength.'

Rollison thought: Golden Boy!

'Did you catch——'

'Steady a minute, sir!' That was the man washing his arm. The door closed on the man who had asked for Grice.

'Hold still, sir...' There was a long pause. 'It's a clean cut, sir—was it a stab?'

'A throw.'

'Just missed the muscle, I'd say. We'll put a bandage on it temporarily.'

'Thanks. Did they catch Golden Boy?'

'The situation was too confused for us to form a conclusion,' said a man who opened the door as Rollison spoke. The voice and the phraseology made identification easy: this was Chief Inspector Jackson. He moved heavily towards the bed. 'How are you?'

'Not bad,' Rollison said. 'They couldn't *all* have got away, could they?'

'We crammed Black Marias full of them,' said Jackson, with satisfaction. 'Mr. Wardle, did you notice anything conspicuous when you came in?'

Rollison said: 'There was a girl in my room—she was conspicuous enough. She was here to find out where the missing tape might be. She was reinforced with four youths, including Golden Boy.'

'So Mr. Grice said,' stated Jackson flatly. 'Perhaps conspicuous was the wrong word to use. I meant, rather, something you noticed that struck you as being out of line.'

A bandage was being wound firmly round Rollison's arm as he tried to see a mental picture of what had happened. Then he remembered one thing he had thought odd.

'Toby's van,' he said.

'The tobacconist wholesaler?'

'Yes.'

'*Very* interesting,' said Jackson, with obvious satisfaction. 'Anything else?'

'No,' said Rollison. 'Except—I didn't think there were so many long-haired louts in London.'

'Nor did I,' confessed Jackson. 'Somewhat alarming that so many could be relied upon to congregate in this vicinity.' He stared at Rollison from the foot of the bed, still showing not the slightest sign of recognition. 'And all for *your* benefit,' he stated almost accusingly. 'They certainly meant to scare the wits out of you.'

'They wanted to impress me, and you, too, I should imagine,' Rollison retorted. 'I thought you were supposed to be watching the place.' For the first time since his rescue he remembered that Ebbutt's men had also been on guard, and a streak of anxiety shot through him.

'We were watching, with three of Ebbutt's prize-fighters,' stated Jackson. 'Then these louts appeared in vans and cars and simply drove everyone out by weight of numbers.'

'How did your chaps get into the warehouse?' demanded Rollison.

'Ah, well, we're prepared for more contingencies than the public give us credit for,' said Jackson smugly. 'Those louts could get away with what they did for half an hour or so, but after that we were bound to move them. Used six fire-fighting tenders with hoses, after the tear gas,' he added with obvious satisfaction. 'Mr. Grice——'

Before he could go on, the door opened and Grice himself came in. The thunderous expression on his face told them what they were anxious to know: they hardly needed to hear him say:

'Golden Boy got away—there's no trace of him at all.' He glared accusingly, at each of the detectives in turn, then went on in a very precise voice: 'I wish to talk to Mr. Wardle alone.'

The detectives who had given Rollison such attention were quick to go but Jackson, to Rollison's surprise, hesitated and stayed until the door had closed on them.

'I have had some discussion with Mr. Wardle, sir——'

'Tell me about it later,' Grice ordered.

Jackson's huge shoulders moved in a shrug, and he went out. The door seemed to shut furiously behind him. If Grice noticed, he ignored it, standing over Rollison like an accusing prophet.

'How long are you going to keep up this charade now?'

'Do I have to make an immediate decision?' asked Rollison. All he wanted was to allow his mind time to rest, and he resented Grice's manner.

'Yes,' said Grice flatly. 'About fifty newspapermen and as many photographers are outside, the street is nearly as jammed with them as it was with the youths. They want to see the mysterious Mr. Wardle. Who are they going to see? Wardle or Rollison?'

CHAPTER FIFTEEN

ARREST

So Grice was right: the decision had to be made now.

Only yesterday, Rollison had been 'murdered'. If the truth were made known now, it would be a farce. There could hardly be a greater sensation than this afternoon's, and to announce his safety would surely be an anti-climax—yes, farce was the word. Yet if he kept up the pretence and was identified it would be almost as ridiculous. There was only one time for the disclosure—when the case was over and Golden Boy in the dock.

Rollison hitched himself up in bed.

'Must I talk to them?'

'If you don't they'll want to know why, and one of them will be sure to guess the reason.' That was probably true. 'And if you talk to them, the chances are fifty to one that they'll see through the disguise.'

'So I can't win,' Rollison said. 'Without help.'

'What do you mean, without help?'

'Your help.'

'Don't you think I've stuck my neck out far enough already?' That gave a clue to Grice's mood, an indication that he would not only feel ridiculous, but be blamed as well, if his share in the deception were known. Rollison stifled a momentary annoyance. Remembering the way Grice had pleaded with him to withdraw from the case, he answered gently:

'Yes, Bill, you have. But it *has* been in a good cause—that of finding Golden Boy. And if you'll forgive the reminder, it was I who got him here, and the police who let him go.'

Grice growled: 'Oh, it worked, I'll grant you that.' He moved away from the bed, stared through the narrow window, and went on: 'What do you want me to do?'

'Arrest Mr. Wardle,' answered Rollison mildly.

Grice spun round, wide eyed.

'Why on earth——' he began, then paused, and gave a little snort of a laugh. 'You really do beat the band,' he said. 'So we are to arrest you and put a blanket over your head in the time-honoured fashion—and hustle you into a police car?'

'That's right.'

'What do we charge you with?'

'You don't have to make a charge until tomorrow, in court.'

'And you stay quietly in the cells at Cannon Row.'

'Oh, no,' Rollison said. '*I* escape. Or you drop the charge.'

Grice laughed again, unwillingly.

'And how do you reappear?' he inquired. 'As Mr. Wardle, or Mr. Rollison?'

'I'll have time to work that out,' Rollison said. 'Bill, don't make such a fuss over this. It's the obvious way—and no one will be suspicious, except possibly Jackson. What's got under *his* skin?'

Grice said: 'He was in charge of watching you and this place. If anyone fell down on the job, he did. Let me tell you something, Rolly. When this is over the one man who will resent being fooled is Jackson. And Jackson doesn't forget.'

'If you're asking me to confide in Jackson, no,' said Rollison. 'He'd give the game away before you could turn round. We can let Jackson take care of himself. Will *he* arrest me?'

'And then you escape? No. I'll leave the arrest to the Divisional men,' Grice decided.

That was how he promised to do what Rollison asked.

'Thanks, Bill,' Rollison said gruffly.

'You'll probably live to hate me for it,' Grice said, 'if you do live. There are two things you ought to know. Long-haired louts have been watching the Marigold Club—you can't go there. They've been watching the hospital where Jolly's likely to be for another week. Your flat's watched even though it's still uninhabitable. Ebbutt's flat above the Blue Dog and his gymnasium are also being watched. In the event of you getting away, where are you going?'

'Are the shops being watched?' asked Rollison.

'Which shops?'

'The Penryns', for instance—or the Slaters'.'

'Jackson didn't say they were,' Grice answered slowly, 'so probably they're not. You couldn't go to the Penryns, but I suppose the Slaters would take a chance.'

'I think they would,' said Rollison.

After a pause, Grice demanded: 'Are you sure you can trust them?'

'I'd rather trust them than anybody,' said Rollison. 'What makes you ask?'

Grice pursed his lips, and was silent for some time. Then he said:

'Rolly, I think you should take into consideration the manner in which Slater flew at you and Jackson, and threatened to use the gun—don't look at me like that!' Grice broke off. 'Just don't take them on trust.'

'Bill,' said Rollison. 'Come clean.'

'There's nothing more to tell you.'

'Come clean,' ordered Rollison. 'Do you mean you think that the Slaters might have been involved with Golden Boy, and for some reason parted company?'

'Yes,' said Grice.

'Evidence?'

'None.'

'Jackson's idea?'

'Yes,' admitted Grice.

'*Very* interesting,' said Rollison. 'And if I wanted a reason for taking the Slaters into my confidence, this is it. I'll go to them and tell them I'm on the run and ask them to hide me. If Jackson's right, then it shouldn't be hard to find out.'

'If Jackson's right, then Slater might buy his way back into Golden Boy's favour by betraying you,' Grice said.

'That's what we're going to find out,' said Rollison, almost light-heartedly. Then his expression changed and he went on in a very different tone: 'How many long-haired louts do you think are involved, Bill?'

'On what we now know, at least three hundred,' Grice said flatly. 'And there might be many more. If each shop which sells the stuff had a hundred customers——' he broke off.

'And if there were a hundred shops you'd have ten thousand customers,' Rollison said. 'It doesn't really matter what chances I take, does it? We've got to get to the bottom of this, without losing a minute.'

Grice said heavily: 'I suppose you're right.'

Events went like clockwork.

Grice announced an impending arrest ... a Divisional Chief Inspector made it, charging 'Robert Wardle' with conspiring to cause a breach of the peace and inciting a number of unnamed youths to violence and resistance to the police ... None among the newspapermen present queried this ... none of the newspapermen were surprised that Wardle proved camera-shy and covered his face when taken to a police car ... The Divisional Police questioned Rollison as if this were a genuine arrest ... Jackson came into the charge-room and put question after question, all obviously implying that Rollison had come to terms with Golden Boy.

At half-past nine, Rollison was released, and hustled out of a side door at the police station in Whitechapel. No one seemed to notice him. He reached a bus stop at a quarter to ten, and caught a departing bus to Chelsea Town Hall.

He walked to the Slaters', and saw a dim light in the back of the shop, a brighter light in the front upper room. He rang the door-bell at the street door, and drew back. Almost at once he saw the light stream out above his head—Slater was trying to see who it was. The light faded. Rollison waited, and nothing happened. Belatedly he realised that he should have telephoned, but there was no telephone kiosk near. He rang again.

This time, he heard footsteps on the stairs. He drew back so that Jack Slater should have no reason to fear being jumped. The door opened an inch or two, and Slater's face appeared—but he did not come out.

'Who's there?' he demanded.

Rollison said urgently: 'I must see you.'

'You can see me when I know what it's all about,' retorted Slater. 'Come closer.'

'You won't recognise me, but——'

'If you want to see me, come closer,' Slater growled.

Rollison drew near. Two cars appeared in the street, and went past, sidelights on. Three youths walked along the other side of the road, immersed in conversation. Rollison drew within a couple of feet of Slater, who said:

'See this?'

He showed the Luger in his hand.

Rollison said in his natural voice: 'That will get you into serious trouble one of these days.'

Slater caught his breath. Rollison did not speak again, simply waited. He had to wait for a long time, but at last he was rewarded.

'It *can't* be,' breathed Slater.

'It is,' Rollison said casually. 'May I come in?'

Slater tried to speak, failed, and tried again. This time he succeeded.

'You're *not* dead!'

'I will be if you leave me out here much longer,' Rollison said. 'I may have been followed.'

'Good God!' There was a scuffle of movement, then a chain dropped and the door opened wide. Rollison stepped through and Slater closed the door. As he did so, Jill called from the landing in a quivering voice:

'Who is it, Jack?'

'A—a friend,' Slater said, unevenly. 'You—you won't be-lieve——' He broke off, looking at Rollison as if at a ghost.

'I'd never have recognised you,' he said. 'It's hard to be-lieve——'

'Don't keep muttering down there!' Jill's words came sharp and ragged. 'Who is it?'

'You've nothing at all to worry about,' Rollison called in his Wardle voice. 'In fact I hope you're going to get a very pleasant surprise.' He started up the stairs as Jack dropped the chain into its slot, and followed. Jill backed away until she was directly beneath the landing light and Rollison could see her clearly.

Why *was* she so terrified?

He spoke quietly, in his own voice: 'I had to fool you so as to fool everyone else, Jill. I'm sorry.'

She stared.

He reached the landing and paused.

Jill stared at him blankly, too astounded to take it in properly.

'It *is* me,' Rollison assured her. 'I've fooled some of my closest friends with this disguise, you're certainly not the only one to be taken in. I'm all right, Jill—really.'

In that moment he actually forgot his bandaged arm.

Jill's face puckered. He remembered the moment when she had burst into tears, and wondered if she was going to break down again, whether her nerves were in such a state that any shock would have affected her in the same way.

Rollison moved forward a pace.

'Jill,' Jack Slater said, 'it *is* the Toff!'

'Oh, thank God you're alive.' Jill flung herself forward and Rollison found himself hugging her, felt her arms almost fiercely tight about him. 'Oh, thank God!' she repeated. 'I couldn't bear it. I simply couldn't bear the fact that you were dead, it was as if we'd killed you.' She strained her shoulders back to stare at him, as if she would not be fully satisfied until her eyes could confirm what her ears told her. 'You are——'

'On my word of honour, I am me,' stated Rollison. 'Jill dear—let my left arm go, will you?'

'Your left——' She sprang back. 'Are you hurt?'

'Not enough to worry about but enough to be painful,' Rollison said, and laughed at the concern which showed in her eyes. 'It's all bandaged, nothing more to be done. It happened in that little skirmish in Wapping this afternoon.'

'Little skirmish!' exclaimed Jack Slater. 'It was a full-scale gang riot—hey! There's a special news report about it on television, in a few minutes. Can you stay?'

Rollison said quietly: 'What I'd like you to do is hide me for a day or two, Jack. I've burned all my boats behind me and I've literally nowhere else to go.'

He half-expected a hearty: 'Yes, of course.' He half-expected Jack to shoot a nervous glance at Jill, before answering 'Gladly,' or something else to that effect. He had not the slightest expectancy of the sudden stillness, the appalled silence, which greeted his words.

CHAPTER SIXTEEN

CONFESSION

ROLLISON waited, without saying a word. It seemed a long time before the others recovered from a shock which had obviously been great. Jill looked across at her husband, Jack put a hand to his forehead and pressed as if his head would fall to pieces if he did not hold it together. Then they both began to speak at the same time.

'Jill——'

'Jack, we must——'

They stopped.

Rollison made himself say: 'Don't worry, I'll find somewhere. I thought you two would like to help.'

'We *would*!'

'Of course we would,' said Jack Slater. 'The only thing is——' he paused, and Jill jumped in as if she couldn't bear another moment's hesitation.

'Someone's coming to see us.'

'And if he turns up——' Jack began.

'Now forget it,' said Rollison. 'It didn't occur to me that you might have visitors. That's the trouble when you get involved in this kind of thing, everything else drops out of the mind. I'll be off.'

He turned towards the head of the stairs.

They actually allowed him to start the descent, and then Jill cried:

'Don't go! Jack, what are you thinking of?'

Jack Slater muttered something under his breath, and it sounded like, 'We'll have to tell him everything.' Rollison took another step, and Jill almost screamed: 'Jack!'

'Mr. Rollison,' Slater called, 'please come back. I know I'm behaving very badly but I think you'll understand why. Jilly love, will you make some coffee? You'd like coffee, Mr. Rollison, wouldn't you?'

'As a matter of fact I'd like a sandwich, if——'

'Of course,' said Jill, more quietly. 'I'll leave the kitchen door open and then I can hear what you're saying.'

They led him into the front room, scene of the Sunday picnic, the ghost of Jolly appearing from a box of opened chocolates—a box that had been in the picnic basket. Jill slipped into the kitchen. Jack pointed to a chair, then took the Luger from his pocket and put it next to the chocolates. He looked pale and on edge. Television seemed to have been forgotten.

'The fact is we've only told you half the truth,' he said.

Shades of Grice and Jackson!

'About what?' asked Rollison, as he sat down.

'This shop and—the whole bloody situation.'

'Care to tell me the whole truth now?'

With a flash of the real man, Slater said: 'Last thing I want to do, really. I like to fight my own troubles.' He began to walk about the room agitatedly. 'As a matter of fact I'm a heel, a downright heel! I should have told you all this before but I thought I might still get something out of it. If it's any consolation, I don't think Jill would have stayed with me. She certainly wouldn't if you'd been dead, I suppose there's a hope now.' He broke off and gave a fierce grin. 'You haven't the faintest idea what I'm talking about, have you?'

'Have *you*?' demanded Rollison.

'Oh, yes—I just don't like confessions so I'm garbling it,' said Slater. 'I've turned my hand to most things and had quite a number of jobs in my time. Among them was driving a van for Toby's—you know, the wholesalers.'

Rollison's eyes widened.

'For how long?'

'Six months or so—long enough to know what *they* were up to. Or to get a pretty good idea, anyhow.'

'What are they up to?'

'Buying stolen goods.'

'The stolen stocks, you mean?'

'That's it,' said Slater, swinging round and standing forbiddingly over the Toff. 'I wasn't sure for a long time, but then I proved it. A carton of cigarettes was sprayed accidentally with paint—it didn't harm the cigarettes—and I delivered it to a shop which that evening had a robbery. Next day, I was delivering the same carton to another.'

Rollison asked: 'What did you do?'

'*Nothing!*' burst out Jill, from the kitchen door. 'That's what started everything. If only you'd gone to the police then——'

'Well, I didn't,' Jack said flatly.

'And look what's happened!'

'Oh, put a sock in it,' rasped Slater. 'This didn't all happen because I kept my mouth shut. The money was good, and I thought it would get better. I was only one driver out of a dozen. So I stayed.'

'What you mean is you thought you could get a share of the filthy money,' said Jill. She came in this time with a laden tray; and on the tray was a bowl of steaming soup, bread, butter, cheese, and biscuits. 'For goodness sake put a table by Mr. Rollison's chair. That's the truth, and the sooner you admit it, the better you'll feel.'

'*You'll* feel, you mean,' growled Slater. He put a small table into position and went on: 'Yes—that's the truth. I'd had a raw deal over my accident at the mine. I decided it was time I got something for nothing.' He obviously expected a comment from Jill, and when it didn't come, he went on: 'I told Jilly I was waiting until I could *really* give a case to the police but she knew what I was up to, really.'

'Blackmail!' murmured Rollison.

Slater growled: 'Do you have to cross the t's and dot the i's?'

'It's neater than disguising the truth with flourishes.'

'All right, then, blackmail, if that's the word you like.' Slater watched as Rollison began to eat. '*I* say I just wanted a bigger cut in what was going. My boss was Bert Williams, and I asked him flat out one day, how much I was going to get for delivering the same cigarettes to three or four different shops. That gave him a hell of a shock, I can tell you.'

'How much did you get?' demanded Rollison.

'Ten quid a week,' answered Slater.

'And wasn't it enough?'

'I daresay I would have gone along with it for a few months,' said Slater, 'but then——' he broke off, looking at his wife, and obviously this was her cue, for she picked up the story immediately.

'An aunt of mine died and left me over a thousand pounds,' she said. 'She'd been ill for a long time, and I'd nursed her for years. I hadn't even realised she had any money but when *this* windfall came, well, it looked wonderful!'

'Enough to buy a business,' said Rollison drily.

'That's right.'

'Be honest, since honesty's the order of the day,' rasped Jack. '*You* thought we'd get a nice discount off supplies if I just kept my mouth shut.' He glared at Jill as if expecting her to deny the charge.

Jill raised her hands and dropped them heavily by her sides.

'I was mad—*mad*,' she whispered.

'That's right. Marital madness. If you must know,' he turned back to the Toff, 'we are two *good* people gone wrong. I'd never stolen a penny in my life and Jill's one of those simple types who leaves her fare with a passenger if the conductor's gone on top. My *God*!' he breathed. 'I got sick to death of honesty.'

'Or of failure,' murmured Rollison.

'What the hell do you mean by that?'

'What I said.'

'But it was one bit of bad luck after another——' Jill began.

'That's what they call it,' Rollison said bitingly. 'The prisons of England are full of people who got there by bits of bad luck. Now before you start bellowing at me or grabbing your Luger, *listen*.' He glared at Slater. 'If this had come off you would have consoled your conscience, wouldn't you?'

'Supposing I would?'

'But it *never* comes off,' Jill said.

'No,' Rollison agreed, more gently. 'People think it does, and for a while it may, but if you're naturally honest it always catches up with you. Now and again, someone's lucky. They not only avoid being found out but they stand a chance of making amends. You two are lucky—if you've got the courage.'

Standing very still, Jack Slater said:

'How?'

'Oh, we *must*!' cried Jill, and she took several short steps forward. 'Just tell us how.'

'Who are you expecting tonight?' Rollison demanded.

'Bert—Bert Williams.'

'Why?'

'He telephoned me and said he had a deal to offer.'

'Before or after the shindig this afternoon?'

'Oh—*after*. Only half an hour before you arrived,' Slater said. 'I was half-afraid it was a trap—that's why I was so careful when you arrived. He'll be here at half-past eleven.'

Rollison asked: 'Where can you hide me?'

'*Hide?*' echoed Slater.

'Up in the loft,' cried Jill. 'I was up there yesterday when you were on the telephone, you can hear every word. And it's easy to get up there—Jack! That's the very place.'

'It's the place all right,' said Slater, but Rollison was not sure whether he was pleased or sorry. 'But if he should find you——'

'Let's worry about that later.'

'*I* worry about it now,' Slater said, bluntly. 'If he knows he's been tricked Golden Boy might kill us both. I'm no loss, but Jill is another matter.'

'Jack——'

'Quiet, woman!'

Jill fell silent. Rollison watched Slater with quickening anxiety, seeing a man torn two ways, and not yet sure which way he would choose. It was a quarter past eleven, so there was no time to spare. Slater's face was set in harsh, unyielding lines, indecision showing no sign in it.

Suddenly, he strode to the television.

'Let's see what they look like *en masse*,' he growled. 'Let's see what they look like. The radio makes them out to be hell-hounds. Let's see what the television people do.' He switched on the 19" screen, then moved away and dropped into a chair, glancing up at Jill and asking brusquely: 'Where's that coffee you talked so much about? Get a move on!'

The television was beginning to make static noises.

A disembodied voice was booming: '...*in London since the General Strike in 1926 ... Estimates vary as to the number of people involved, but it was enough to cause the Riot Squads of the Metropolitan Police, including the Thames Division, to turn out in full strength...*'

The picture came on, and Rollison caught his breath.

Every approach to the Docks Hotel was a seething mass of youths; he saw again what he had seen with the naked eye, but now all the colours were a uniform grey. Yet this did not lessen the intensity of the scene or take away from the vicious-ness so horribly apparent in the expressions and attitudes of the youths. The pictures were blurred and not too steady, but of the unbridled savagery there could be no doubt whatsoever.

'There you are,' exclaimed Jill.

The two men had been so intent on the screen that they had not seen her come in. She stood with the tray of coffee in her hands just behind her husband's chair. She was quivering and the spoons were rattling slightly in the saucers.

Rollison saw himself as Wardle.

There was Golden Boy, too—in front of him, apparently helpless.

There was movement at his lips and at Golden Boy's and Rollison could recall every word, could remember the near-terror with which he had realised that if he defied Golden Boy and broke his arm, the youths near him *would* tear him to pieces.

He was profoundly thankful that his face was expressionless; at least he was not showing his fear.

The picture changed and showed police at one of the warehouse loading bays, their tear gas guns at the ready. Other shots showed police hemmed in doorways and at street corners. Suddenly Rollison saw the smoke from the guns, saw himself struck, saw himself fall. For a dreadful instant it looked as if he would be trampled underfoot, but other shells were fired, panic took hold of the crowd near him, and those who were on the fringe of the gas began to turn back. There were shots of him being taken into the Docks Hotel, then a switch and a change in the tone of the announcer's voice.

'All this time mounted police had been gathered near Wapping High Street, and at a signal from Superintendent Grice of Scotland Yard, they began to ride at walking pace towards the main scene of the disturbance. At the same time fire-engines, firemen with hoses at the ready, approached from the other direction ...'

There were shots of the uniformed police on their fine horses, shots of the six fire-engines, in line, manned by steel-helmeted men with their horses. Suddenly the water sprayed out from the hoses and swamped the youths already struggling to get away from the tear gas. In the side streets Black Marias could be seen, their back doors open, and as the youths rushed to escape, police were pushed to one side and bowled over. More and more police arrived, wielding their truncheons, and now dozens of the youths were thrust into the Black Marias.

Abruptly, Slater said: 'You're right, Toff. No one has a chance against an organisation like the police. Still want to hide in the attic?'

'As soon as I've had my coffee,' Rollison said.

CHAPTER SEVENTEEN

THE OFFER

ROLLISON had two cups of coffee, and was standing on the landing beneath the hatch which led into the attic, when the front door bell rang. Slater, holding a ladder against one side of the hatch, said sharply:

'He's here.'

Rollison started to go up, keeping his left arm close to his body. Before the night was out, that arm might cause a lot of trouble. He saw the dim light on in the attic, reached floor level, and began to haul himself over.

'Hurry!' breathed Slater.

'You go and open the door,' urged Jill. 'I'll put the ladder away.'

The bell rang again.

Rollison scrambled into the attic, and almost as soon as he was inside, Jill took the ladder away. He peered down, to see her staring up at him, very pale, and to see Jack Slater's back as he went down the stairs.

'Put the hatch down!' called Jill.

She was in terror.

Rollison placed the hatch cover into position very slowly. It was a long drop—not one that would worry him with two sound arms, but as he was, it would be difficult to get down unaided, and virtually impossible to do so silently.

He heard a voice: 'Hallo. You took your time.'

'You're early.'

'Maybe a minute,' said the caller. 'Don't get the wind up, no one's with me.'

'Since when do I take your word for anything?' demanded Slater.

Footsteps sounded on the stairs, chairs were being moved about in the living-room; one thing at least was certain: sounds did travel very clearly. They were loud as the two men passed immediately beneath the hatch.

Rollison moved with extreme care. He should have come up here before, he had taken too long. There was a cushion and a low stool against a beam, and the floor was boarded over. He tiptoed to the stool and lowered himself cautiously.

'What will you have?' Slater was asking.

'Scotch and water.'

There was the clink of glass on glass, and Rollison wondered what would happen if Slater, by an expressive upward nod, gave him away. There simply wasn't a chance of getting out. He tightened his lips as Slater said:

'Well, what's the offer this time?'

'You've got another chance,' said Bert Williams.

'Maybe I'm giving *him* another chance,' jeered Slater. It did not seem to matter whom he talked to, he soon lapsed into a mood of aggression.

'Listen, Slater,' Williams said in a voice so soft Rollison had to strain his ears to catch the words, 'you'll go too far. He's jumping mad, and he hasn't much time for you, any-way.'

'Then what's he want me for?'

'To do one job,' said Williams.

'What do I get if I do it?'

'You get a thousand pounds without trouble,' Williams said.

Jill exclaimed: 'A thousand *pounds*!'

'If you want to sit in on this, you keep quiet,' Slater growled at her. 'When do I get the thousand?'

'I've got half of it here. You get the rest when the job's done.'

After a long pause, Slater asked gruffly:

'What's the job?'

'You put one man away,' said Williams carefully.

'You mean—*kill*!' gasped Jill.

Rollison thought: I don't like this at all. Why are they talking in front of her? They must feel quite sure she won't give anything away. The whole tone of the discussion was wrong and he felt more and more uneasy.

'What man?' asked Slater, as if the job itself was hardly worth a second thought.

And then Williams said: 'Rollison. The Toff.'

'How did you know he was alive?' cried Jill Slater.

Rollison thought: They'll tell him at any moment, now.

Jill's voice had faded, neither of the men had spoken since her outburst. The silence seemed to go on for a long time, before Williams drew in an audible breath and spoke very softly:

'Do *you* know he is?'

'He telephoned, a couple of hours ago,' Slater said. It was good for a spur of the moment improvisation, although it might not prove to be good enough.

'So he telephoned,' echoed Williams. 'What did he want?'

'Sanctuary,' said Slater, and the word seemed strange on his lips. 'He's got nowhere to go.'

'What did you say? Is he—my God, is he coming here?'

'He will if I say so,' answered Slater. 'He's going to call again at twelve midnight.' He was saying all this as if he had rehearsed it—a surprising man indeed. 'Want me to invite him?'

'It would be perfect,' Williams breathed. 'Then you could fix him—and don't worry about the body, we'll look after that.'

'No body,' said Slater flatly.

'What's that?' Williams was startled.

'I said—no body. I'm not killing Rollison or anyone else, you can tell Golden Boy that.'

'But he'll have your——'

'Shut up and listen to me,' said Jack Slater. 'I'm not a killer and I'm not going to start being one. I don't know what is between Golden Boy and the Toff, but it's none of my business. If I get the Toff here I want five thousand pounds *and* the shop—and if there's any monkey business I'll go to the police.'

'You can't make terms with Goldy like that!'

'Yes I can,' said Slater. 'I'll get the Toff here—and then Goldy can do his own dirty work.'

'He'll never come *here*.'

'Then he won't get the Toff, will he,' Slater said. 'My terms are these: Five thousand pounds, which Goldy is to bring in person. Then, when Goldy's here, and not a minute before, I'll arrange for the Toff to come.'

Williams said unbelievingly: 'It's suicide. If he knows you can get the Toff, but won't, he'll——'

'Not with a lady present. Go and tell him,' ordered Slater. 'And you can also tell him I'm not going to weaken. I've had enough of being pushed around. Tell him to telephone me, yes or no.'

Williams seemed to let out a long, slow sigh.

'Well, you can't say I haven't warned you.' There was a pause and then a tense laugh. 'You've got guts, I will say that for you.' There was a scraping of chairs. 'Okay, I'll get going.' Footsteps followed, very loud beneath the hatch—Slater was seeing the other man out. As their footsteps grew quieter, Jill's became more and more audible in the room below. Rollison stood up and went to the hatch but did not open it. He heard whispering voices from the foot of the stairs, or what sounded like whispering. Slater *could* be making a fresh deal. The street door slammed and Slater came running up; there was only one set of footsteps, Rollison felt sure of that. They stopped beneath the hatch and in a voice of restrained excitement, Slater called:

'You awake?'

Rollison pushed back the hatch.

'I'm awake all right—and Williams certainly didn't catch *you* asleep, did he?'

'Not a chance,' said Slater, looking up. 'What did you think of the performance?'

'Remarkably effective.'

'Jack, you were wonderful!' Jill came hurrying, delighted. Slater put an arm round her and gave her a fierce hug.

'That's my baby! A reprieve for Jack Slater, villain, yet— or do I mean redemption?'

'Do you think he'll come?' demanded Jill, eagerly.

'He'll come all right,' said her husband, confidently. 'The trouble is he'll probably bring a small army with him—he won't want to be fooled again in life or in death.' Slater laughed in an excited manner, then moved to get the ladder. 'Want any help, or can you make it on your own?'

Rollison said : 'I'm not coming down yet.'

'*What!*'

'I'm staying where I'm comparatively safe,' Rollison insisted. 'If I were to go out now, I would almost certainly be shot in a dozen places, if not torn to pieces.'

'But Williams was alone!'

'He came in alone,' Rollison said. 'I'm not——'

'You're coming down if I have to drag you down,' Slater said. 'If he comes and finds you here, he'll know I've lied to him.'

'Yes, won't he?'

There was a long, tense silence—broken harshly by the ringing of the telephone. Jill backed away, into the living-room; the bell went on ringing. Slater glared up, as if he were coming to realise that there was virtually no way in which he could make Rollison come down.

The telephone stopped.

'Yes,' said Jill. 'Who? *Who?* Well, I—I don't think ... I mean I don't understand, I thought he was ... Well, I'll ask my husband.' There was a ting as she put down the telephone and almost at once she came to the doorway, staring up at Rollison. 'It's Superintendent Grice,' she said. 'For you.'

Grice was the one man who knew where he was—the one man who knew he had come to confide in the Slaters and so might well ask for Rollison by name. Yet Rollison hesitated. It *could* be a trick—a way of getting him out of the attic—or at least a way of finding out if he was alive and *was* with the Slaters.

'Come on down,' Slater ordered.

'Get his home telephone number and tell him I'll call him back,' Rollison said.

'He said he was calling from Scotland Yard,' said Jill.

'You won't know whether that's the truth or not until you come down,' Slater insisted. 'You might as well make up your mind to it. And you can have a police bodyguard in the street so that you won't be mown down by Goldy's boys.'

Rollison drew back from the hatch and turned his back.

'Put the ladder into position,' he said.

'*That's* more like it.' He heard the ladder being moved and felt the top of it touch the back of his right heel. 'I'm holding it,' Slater called.

Rollison went down slowly and cautiously until he reached the floor. Slater patted him on his left shoulder and pain shot through him agonisingly. He gritted his teeth and went into the big room, not by any means sure that the caller was Grice. He picked up the receiver.

'This is Reginald Wardle,' he said.

'Richard Rollison is good enough for me,' said Grice. There wasn't the slightest doubt that it was he. 'I'm glad you're still alive.'

'Did you expect me to be otherwise?' asked Rollison.

'Yes,' said Grice. 'I've just learned that Slater drove a van for Toby's—and we've raided Toby's warehouse tonight.' Rollison felt a stab of surprise at that news; it was always somehow surprising that the police would do things of which he hadn't the slightest knowledge. 'And we found plenty,' Grice went on in a tone of deepest satisfaction. 'Stolen goods from at least ten shops were there—the fingerprints of the original owners have been identified. We also know how the drug is distributed.'

'You *found* some?'

'We found very big supplies,' stated Grice. 'It's in bottles of sweets called *Sherbert Suckers*. They're sold in small quantities for children but the bottles which contain LSD and heroin are specially marked. We haven't the whole story yet but we do know that we've stopped the main method of distribution, and we *think* the supplies come into the Port of London off Dutch ships and are transferred straight to Toby's warehouse.'

'Fascinating,' observed Rollison. He saw both the Slaters out of the corner of his eye; they seemed intent only on watching him. 'Why tell me about this now?'

'There's no doubt at all—the Slaters are involved,' said Grice. 'I want to get you out of there as soon as I can. I'll send——'

'Hold it,' interrupted Rollison. 'Have you caught Golden Boy?'

'We will.'

'*Have* you actually got him?'

'No, but——'

'Or the organisers of the whole series of crimes?' asked Rollison.

'Not yet, but——'

'I'll stay here,' Rollison said. 'I'm supposed to be having an appointment with Golden Boy sometime in the next hour. Want to make sure I'm not killed, Bill?'

Grice's voice sounded almost husky as he said: 'More than anything else.'

'Then keep your men away from here,' Rollison said very clearly. 'If Golden Boy knows the place is watched he'll know he's walking into a trap. If it's *not* watched he'll come.'

'And *you'll* be in the trap,' Grice snapped. 'Rolly, haven't you the sense to know that they're out to get you?'

'Yes,' said Rollison.

'You *knew* that?'

'It has become increasingly obvious,' Rollison said, 'that my head on a platter is a main objective. I want to find out why. I'm *going* to find out why,' he added. 'Keep your men away, Bill, and make sure Ebbutt's aren't in the vicinity, either.'

CHAPTER EIGHTEEN

GOLDEN BOY

As Rollison put down the receiver, acutely conscious of having burned his boats, Jack Slater went to the window and looked out. He beckoned. Rollison joined him. The street appeared to be empty. Within sight were three lamps, all burning brightly, adding sparkle to the clear night. Two yellow squares of windows where someone was still up, showed further along the street.

'You've gone halfway,' urged Slater. 'Go the whole hog, Toff.'

'But there might be men waiting in doorways or round the corner,' Jill remarked in a very subdued voice.

'I did a deal with Williams,' Slater said. 'I think he'll play it straight because it's the only way Goldy can be sure of getting what he wants.'

He talked of 'Goldy' as the prisoner 'Mick' had done; and he talked as if he were wholly familiar with the situation, had not simply been caught up in it and tried to turn it to his own advantage. He was on edge, but eager; Jill was obviously troubled.

Rollison said: 'If I go out there and I'm attacked——'

'Listen,' said Slater, 'if I'd simply wanted to let Williams kill you, you would be dead by now.'

Yes, thought Rollison. Yes, that was true enough. A dozen questions burned themselves into his mind but this wasn't the time to ask them. It was a time for decision. He let the curtain fall at the window, and moved towards the door.

'I hope you've a conscience,' he said.

'Jack——' began Jill, in obvious distress.

'It will be all right,' Slater insisted, and put a restraining arm round her shoulders. 'Will you telephone half an hour from now, Toff?'

'Yes.' Rollison went out on to the landing, glanced up at the open loft and avoided the ladder, then went down the stairs. As he reached the door he took a small automatic from his pocket, reflecting that no one had searched him. His only other weapon was a knife, clipped to his right arm, and three more of the cigarettes—but none of Golden Boy's men was going to let him get away with the cigarette trick again.

He opened the door: cold air swept in.

There was no porch, no shelter, once he stepped outside— only the certain knowledge that Golden Boy wanted him dead.

He stepped on to the pavement, and pulled the door behind him.

Nothing happened; there were no nearby sounds, only distant noises of traffic. The night was still, and moonless, but the cold stars gave light. He turned towards the river, watching each corner, sensing that each breath might be his last.

He reached the corner. Just round it, a couple stood against the wall; lovers.

A car passed, its headlights on, and shone upon a fair-haired girl and a dark-haired youth whose bodies seemed to merge into one and who were quite oblivious of cars or passers-by. Rollison passed them. Along this narrow street there were cars parked close together, doorway after unlit doorway, a dozen places where evil-doers could hide.

No one appeared.

No one attacked.

He could not be sure that no one watched, but certainly no one followed.

He reached the north side of the Embankment and then crossed the empty roadway. To the right the arc of a traffic light was like a warning of disaster. A car, headlights on but dipped, raced along much too fast; a man and girl were silhouettes against Embankment lights, and they seemed as close together as the couple near the shop. Rollison crossed the road and reached the parapet of the Embankment. No ships moved but some boats were moored. Across the river a few of the fairy lights of Battersea Park showed, bright and varied. In one direction there was the spidery span of the Albert Bridge, on the other the wedge of Battersea. Light from the stars and reflected light in the skies showed the monstrous shape of Battersea Power Station, silently belching its gigantic mushrooms of smoke.

Footsteps sounded, heavy, deliberate, distant. Rollison glanced towards the right and saw a policeman approaching.

He drew level, and passed.

'Good evening, sir.'

'Good evening,' Rollison said. 'A lovely night.'

'Yes, sir—one of the best. Can I help you at all?'

'Not unless you can help me reflect on life.'

'Very conducive to reflection, the Thames,' remarked the policeman sagely. 'Goodnight, sir.'

'Goodnight.'

Rollison watched the sturdy figure out of sight, then glanced at his watch. How slowly time could pass; he had been out of the shop for only ten minutes. Would it be best to go and watch and so find out whether anybody went there, and if so, how many? He would have to leave again so as to telephone, he would only be teasing himself. The faint light of a telephone kiosk showed on the other side of the road. He strolled towards it. He was very tired, which wasn't surprising, and he did not really trust his mind to react quickly enough. He told himself that he was crazy to handle this situation on his own—and a moment later told himself that he would be crazy not to.

At last, the half an hour passed.

He stepped into the kiosk, dialled the number, heard the pips, then heard Slater's voice.

'Is that you, Toff?'

Rollison pressed his coin in. 'Yes.'

'He's here,' announced Slater. 'I shouldn't keep him waiting.'

Rollison put down the receiver and stepped out briskly, all sense of tiredness gone. He had never known a situation like this before—perhaps Grice was right and it would be the last he would ever encounter. 'Nonsense!' he muttered, and slipped the gun into a more convenient position, flexing the muscles of his right arm until he felt the knife coming down slowly, the handle touching the palm of his hand.

The lovers had gone.

He turned into the street and saw no one. There were cars and doorways and the menace of darkness—but no one was in sight. The light from the window above the shop seemed very bright.

If *he* were doing what Golden Boy was supposed to be doing, he would have to feel absolutely sure that he would come to no harm; so, the chances were that Golden Boy *did* feel sure.

He must, then, have absolute and implicit faith in the Slaters.

Rollison reached the side door and pressed the bell; and his finger hardly seemed to be off the bell-push before footsteps sounded on the stairs; if Slater wasn't careful, he thought grimly, he would fall down them in his eagerness to get him inside.

The door opened.

'My God, it *is* you!' he exclaimed. 'I didn't think you'd have the guts to come.'

He stood aside for Rollison to pass.

Rollison started up the stairs very slowly. Voices sounded above. The door closed behind him with a note of absolute finality. As he reached the landing he heard a woman laugh: it was not Jill Slater. Slater caught his left arm and pain stabbed through it—but not enough to distract his attention from that laughter and the pleasant voice which followed it.

'Oh, he'll get the surprise of his life.'

Yes, Rollison thought stupidly: the surprise of my life.

'Don't weaken,' urged Slater, and let him go.

Rollison gritted his teeth against the pain, and stepped into the living-room.

Over by the window, where the curtains were drawn, was his niece Geraldine. Sitting back in an armchair, one leg draped over an arm, was his nephew, George. Both were looking intently at him, and although George was smiling broadly there was something very set in his smile.

Geraldine said with strained brightness:

'Hallo, Uncle Richard.'

'Hi, Uncle Toff,' said George.

That was the instant when everything dropped into place; when it needed no more telling why killing him had become a main objective, why the affair had all the appearance of a personal vendetta. It *was* a personal vendetta; the climax of a family feud.

'Look at him,' said Geraldine. 'He really is quite shocked.'

'Push up a chair for Uncle Toff,' said George. 'If you don't he'll collapse before our very eyes, and that could make him feel ridiculous.'

Slater pushed a chair behind the Toff's legs.

'Not ridiculous,' he said.

'No? Then what?'

'The obvious word is "ashamed",' said Rollison in a voice which quivered slightly. 'But there's another.'

'Do tell us, Uncle Richard,' invited Geraldine with mock humility.

'Repulsed,' Rollison said. 'Or perhaps repelled.'

'Wouldn't "appalled" do better?' suggested George. 'After all, to think you have villains in the family! You couldn't possibly live with the shame of it, could you?'

'I could live,' said Rollison. 'I doubt if your mother could. I'm nearly sure it would kill Old Glory.'

'Dear, dear Glory,' sneered George. 'I wonder if you ever realised how much I disliked you, Uncle Toff. And Old Glory. And all the sick-making moralising and the dismal do-good-ing. And having you both held up as shining examples.'

'Ah,' said Rollison, and at last he sat down.

'Tired, Uncle Toff?' asked George.

Rollison said quietly: 'Very tired, but not too tired to hear you out.'

'Well that's good, since you're here to listen, and since you won't be able to tell anyone else. You won't get away with a fake death again, you can be sure of that.'

'Once is enough,' Rollison said.

'It even fooled me for a few hours, but when I heard from the chap you so amusingly call Golden Boy, my second in command, how Mr. Wardle behaved and talked, I began to have doubts. Not many men would have either the courage or the resource to do what you did there, I will say that for you.'

'Well, well,' said Rollison drily, 'should I be flattered?'

'When I was very young I used to look up to you,' George went on. 'And then my father needed a little financial help and you turned him down. Do you remember that, Uncle?'

'I remember very well,' said Rollison. 'I'm beginning to understand better, now. Inherited vice could explain you.'

'I shed no tears for my dead papa,' said George, 'but don't carry the insults too far. That was when my disillusion began —when I began to see the situation from the other side.'

'Ah,' said Rollison again. 'And when did Geraldine begin to see it, George?'

'Not long after me,' George answered. 'Twins think very much alike, you know.'

'So I'm told,' murmured Rollison. 'You both saw the ad-vantage of a life of crime. Is that it?'

'The advantages and the possibilities,' answered George. 'We knew that people were like sheep, we knew that all they needed was a strong lead, and we soon learned how to lead them.'

'Of course, feeding them drugs helped,' said Rollison, sardonically.

'There's money in drugs,' retorted George. 'Uncle dear, let us get one thing clear beyond all possible shadow of doubt. I see no harm in drugs. They *help* us to live. The world you and your smug friends have made for us isn't worth living in, but with a little help from the right drugs one can make believe it is, for a while.'

'It isn't that we don't see any harm in drugs,' said Geraldine. 'We see a lot of good in them. And we don't overcharge, do we George?'

'We make a living, not a fortune,' her brother answered. 'Uncle dear—are you beginning to understand?'

'I understand very well,' Rollison said. 'Your father had delusions of power, it would seem to be an inheritable trait. You've used drugs to make your dupes do what you want them to. The poor fools are afraid that if they don't do what they're told, they won't get their shots or their pills. So they come to heel.'

'How clever of you to guess,' agreed George. He looked young and relaxed—and happy. Geraldine had lost most of her tension, too. She was sitting on the arm of her brother's chair—twins with a combined age of forty-one. It was the more hideous because they were so attractive.

'They won't come to heel any more,' Rollison said. 'The sources of supply have dried up.'

'Yes,' George said. 'Thanks to you.'

His expression changed; a vicious gleam showed in his eyes and his hands clenched; for a moment Rollison thought he would launch himself forward bodily; but somehow he resisted.

'That's the way you've lived,' he said. 'And that's the way you'll die. A smug hypocrite.'

For the first time since this bizarre conversation had begun, Jill Slater interrupted.

'*Hypo*crite? Surely not.'

'Don't let him fool you,' George sneered. 'He thrives on the power his reputation gives him, he loves kicking the other fellow around, he makes plenty out of his lone-wolf act. He's as dependent on crime as any criminal—he thrives on it. Don't let Uncle Toff Rollison fool you. He happens to be smooth enough to keep in with the law, he gets as big a kick out of it as anyone. Your life wouldn't be worth living without crime, would it?'

The Toff returned his vicious gaze quite calmly.

'You're as warped in thinking as any criminal I've ever known,' he said. 'You don't make any sense at all.'

'Don't you believe it,' George declared. 'I make plenty of sense. When we leave here, you'll be dead—and only the Slaters will know that Golden Boy is simply a stooge, that your neglected nephew is the hero of the piece. The drug distribution has stopped, but that was always a short-term business. The shops are owned by those I have put in charge—they'll do a good trade and I'll get a good percentage. We will have built a sound commercial business which no one can take away. Bert Williams will be sent down, like the rest of the active workers—just we four will control Toby's and the shops. No one can pin anything on us. If *that* doesn't make sense, I'd like to know what does?' Very slowly and deliberately, George stood up and moved towards the Toff. 'There's one other thing,' he said. 'If you'd kept your nose out of the business it's just possible you mightn't have had to die. Once you came in, however, what would have been a mere pleasure became a duty—a congenial one, I admit.'

Rollison said: 'From you, as I see you now, a perfectly understandable sentiment. Don't bother to explain it. What matters is whether the Slaters are going to be fool enough to be taken in by you. They'll be accessories to murder—if you kill me, and that will mean prison for life.'

He looked at Jack and Jill Slater, in turn.

'You have to decide whose side you're on,' he said. 'Theirs
—or your own?'

Jill began to cry.

Her tears were enough. Rollison did not need any other
answer to his question.

CHAPTER NINETEEN

JILL SLATER WEEPS

THE other three young people were staring intently at Rollison as if half-fearful of what he would do next. Slater was within reach of the Luger, and George had his hand in his pocket, but none of them moved.

'There's one thing,' Slater said. 'Jill will weep for you.'

'She needs to weep for you,' Rollison retorted.

'Smart words won't help you now,' Slater said harshly.

'Nor will clever tricks such as blowing tear-gas phials out of cigarettes,' said George. 'How many of those cigarettes have you got left?'

'Three,' said Rollison, flatly.

'They'll make interesting trophies for our wall,' gibed George. 'What's the great Toff going to do now that he's cornered? Back against the wall stuff and all that kind of thing, I suppose, working a knife down from the forearm in that neat way you showed me when I was knee high, or do you intend to use a palm gun?'

Rollison said evenly: 'I'm not going to do a thing.'

'The *Toff* wouldn't give in without a fight,' said Geraldine. 'You must be the mysterious Mr. Wardle after all.'

Jill was crying . . .

'The knife's on his right arm,' Slater said. 'The gun's in his waistband so that he can get it easily with his right hand.'

'Geraldine, go and get them,' said George. 'We'll watch him.'

Geraldine moved lightly and easily, smiling her innocent smile close to Rollison's face. He smelt the subtle perfume she wore, could hardly believe that such a dainty little creature could be playing a part in this deadly game. But she was. She opened his jacket and took out the gun, then loosened the clip round his arm through the sleeve, so that the knife fell—and it stuck, quivering, in the floor.

Geraldine backed away.

'Whoever would have believed the Toff would let himself be killed, without a fight,' marvelled Slater. 'I hate shooting a sitting target.'

'A little foolish to boast about an event that is unlikely to take place,' said Rollison lightly. 'Looking a fool must be so depressing.'

Jill was still sobbing.

'Did you hear what he said?' asked Geraldine, as if she were a little alarmed.

'He has to say *something*,' George muttered, but he was uneasy.

'Give me one good reason why we shouldn't,' said Slater.

'You daren't,' answered Rollison blandly.

'Daren't? We've killed——'

'I don't want any confession,' Rollison interrupted sharply. 'You're nauseating enough as it is. You aren't going to kill me because you daren't. George—didn't your friend Micky pass on a message?'

'Message?' demanded Slater. 'What's all this?'

George said slowly: 'You were lying.'

'Oh, no,' said Rollison. 'I wasn't lying then and I'm not lying now. And there's no way you can prove it unless you do kill me.' He glanced at Jill, who had paused in her sobbing, and went on: 'I taped some notes before I was attacked at the Carilon Club, and put the tape safely away. The police will have it in the morning.'

George roared: 'It's a lie!'

'It's the truth,' Rollison said.

'Why, I'll break your neck——'

Jill was sobbing again, as if this were too much for her to bear.

'But you didn't know *we* were involved,' Geraldine said, waspishly. 'It *is* a lie!'

'When the police hear the tape they will learn that I was wondering very early on why I was being singled out,' Rollison said. 'And wondering, too, how it was my flat was broken into with such ease and knowledge. I listed——'

'Stop him!' screamed Geraldine, as if this were too much to bear.

George said: 'Take his left arm, Slater, and give it a twist. That'll make him tell the truth.'

Rollison said as if weary: 'It's the truth, even if I can't make you believe it.' He felt Slater touch his left wrist, and until that moment he had been so unresisting that Slater was obviously unprepared for any counter attack.

Rollison back-heeled, savagely. His heel caught Slater on the shin and sent him staggering backwards, squealing with the pain which had come so suddenly. Rollison rammed his right hand into George's stomach and George, coming forward, had the full power of the blow heightened by his own movement. He staggered back, completely off balance, and Rollison sprang towards the door.

Geraldine fired at him.

Geraldine, sweet pretty twin, levelled his own gun and fired, and she was so close that she couldn't miss. The bullet thudded into his left shoulder jarring his whole body. At the same time, George sprang towards him, livid with rage, while Jack Slater called in a pain-wracked voice:

'There's no tape, he couldn't have made a tape!'

'*Make him talk!*' screamed Geraldine. 'Do something, make him tell the truth.'

'If you two aren't out of the country by tomorrow morning, the police will be on your doorstep,' Rollison said steadily, but he knew that it was a waste of words. They did not want to believe him and so they would not believe him—they would come near to tearing him to pieces in order to make him confess that he had lied. He hadn't a chance, now. Pain was tearing like an animal with savage fangs at his shoulder and he was losing blood fast.

The two men drew close to him. He could see no mercy in their faces, no relenting in their eyes. It was a miserable, futile ending to a strange case. His strangest. Well, the worst he could suffer now was pain. If he told them the truth—that there *was* no tape—they could not be sure whether to believe him or not, and in any case they would not let him go.

There was a strange silence.

He could not hear the men breathing; he could not hear Geraldine screeching her wild orders—what a vixen she was, how near the primitive. He could hear nothing—not even Jill Slater's sobbing.

He backed against the wall, and knew that if the men as much as touched him he would slide down it. They were close together, different and yet so alike in their expressions—evil men, who had fooled him. Geraldine's face, twisted in rage, showed between them.

They had only to stretch out——

'Don't touch him,' gasped Jill Slater in a strange voice. 'Let him go.'

She was out of sight, behind the trio.

Jack Slater snarled: 'Shut your trap!' without even glancing over his shoulder.

'Don't touch him,' Jill repeated, 'or I'll shoot.'

Shoot?

All three turned round to look at her, and as they did so Rollison saw her standing against the far wall, with the Luger in her hands; in *both* hands. Her face was deathly pale: mask-like. Her slender body was a-tremble, and the gun unsteady too, but she kept all three of them covered and for a moment they did not move.

'Go,' she gasped to Rollison. 'Go and get the police.'

The door was only a few feet away.

But he pictured what would happen to her if he left her alone with them; he could not do so, even for a moment. She was near the telephone—but she wasn't composed enough to cover them with the gun in one hand, and dial the police with the other.

Slater said in an icy voice: 'Put that gun down.'

'Go away!' Jill cried to Rollison. 'I can't hold it much longer!'

'*Put that gun down!*' ordered Slater, and he took a step towards her.

She squeezed the trigger and the gun roared.

There would never be any certainty that she had fired deliberately. Her fingers might well have been so unsteady that she pulled without fully realising what she was doing.

The bullet struck her husband in the chest.

Rollison could not see his face, only the horror on hers, but he could see him slump slowly forward, then begin to crumple up. There was such numbed astonishment on the faces of the others that he knew he had an instant of time left.

The small gun was loose in Geraldine's hand.

He screwed himself up to make the effort, moved to her, and took it—and she realised too late what she had allowed him to do. On that instant Jill dropped the gun and ran to Jack, catching her breath, while Rollison backed towards the door, covering his niece and nephew with the little gun.

'Uncle!' cried Geraldine. 'Let us go—we'll leave the country, let us go!'

'Telephone the police,' he ordered, 'or I'll shoot you.'

'But you can't let them arrest us. Think of the scandal, think of the family!' She was coming forward, very slowly. 'Just let us go.'

'Uncle Richard,' George said with an effort, 'it won't do any good to—have us arrested. It's all over now. Let—let us go.'

'For the family's sake——' Geraldine began, and she edged a little nearer.

They were going to jump him, of course; it was their only hope. Plead with him long enough to get close and then rush at him together. He had no doubt of what they meant to do.

Geraldine was very beautiful.

George was startlingly handsome.

And they were both so young.

'Please, Uncle Rolly,' Geraldine said. 'Let us go. We've the flight already booked, no one will be any the worse off.'

Rollison said in a very clear voice: 'If you don't turn round and telephone the police, I shall shoot you.'

Geraldine's eyes looked positively enormous; huge, limpid violets.

'Rolly, *please*——'

She took another step forward and George was poised to spring.

Rollison shot his nephew in the shoulder, and saw him flinch and gasp and back away. He saw Geraldine's expression turn from one of sweet, pleading innocence into that of a virago, and he prayed she would not attack him.

Then there came a thunderous banging on the door at the foot of the stairs, and the sound of voices raised. It so shocked Geraldine that she faltered, and gave Rollison time to move out of the room and on to the landing. He could not summon the strength to go down and open the door, they would have to break it down.

He heard a familiar voice, crying: 'Open this door, in the name of the law. Open this door.' Only Chief Inspector Jackson could give that command in exactly that way.

The banging was repeated.

Geraldine was in the room staring down at her brother. Jill was crouched on her knees by the side of her dead husband.

Then the police began to break the door down . . .

CHAPTER TWENTY

SECOND SIGHT?

'IF you want to know where you are,' said Grice, 'you're in the nursing home where your Mr. Wardle was born, but you're registered as Richard Rollison. Ninety-four newspapermen of thirty-two nationalities are waiting to interview you—not because you're you or you performed miracles, but because they thought you were dead and you are alive. Do you *feel* alive?' added Grice, with rare if barbed humour.

'I know I am,' said Rollison. 'I can hear and see you.'

Grice smiled.

'You'll be all right. To the last you were lucky—that bullet chipped but didn't fracture the bone.'

'To the nearly last, you mean,' said Rollison. 'When did it happen?'

'The day before yesterday.'

'So they put me under sedation.'

'They decided you needed complete rest for a while and there was no other way to make sure of it.'

'No doubt I'm a suspicious mortal,' said Rollison, 'but I smell the influence of my Aunt Gloria.'

'You're quite right,' said Grice. 'You were brought here and she came to see you. You gave her a garbled version of what had happened, and I filled in the rest. You will probably be interested in her reaction.'

'I can tell you her reaction,' Rollison said. 'That Georgina should never have married Arthur. Then she went off to comfort Georgina, who was feeling very sorry for herself.'

Grice was startled into a laugh.

'You'll live!' he said. 'She's a remarkable woman. Lady Hurst, I mean. She has arranged for the defence, of course.

George and Geraldine were charged with attempted murder at
the West London Court this morning, and they were remanded
for a week.'

Rollison caught his breath. 'Jill?'

'Need you ask. Running the shop with Ebbutt's men by day,
staying with your aunt at night. I don't know a lot about her,'
went on Grice, 'but I think she's lucky to be rid of Slater so
early in the marriage—I think she'll be all right.'

Rollison said gruffly: 'If anyone can help her, Aunt Gloria
can.' He was almost morosely silent for a few minutes, then
went on: 'Bill—why did Jackson come when he did?'

'He unearthed evidence that Slater knew about the drugs,
one of the prisoners from the Wapping riot talked. So he
called me for authority to come and arrest Slater. I told him to
make it swift and take no chances. I was worried enough about
your trust in Slater, and this clinched it.'

'Just as well you acted when you did,' Rollison said. 'I had a
suspicion that Jackson didn't regard me with full approval.'

'He didn't, but he does now. I had a long talk with him,'
Grice added. 'He wouldn't tell me what he thought to begin
with, only what he thinks now. I gather there is a considerable
change, not to say volte-face.'

Rollison smiled wryly. 'Did you suspect the truth?'

'I hadn't the faintest idea,' Grice answered.

'You were *very* insistent that I should drop out,' said Rollison. 'Why was that? Second sight?'

'I can only say I had a most uneasy feeling,' Grice said.
'Let's leave it at that. There is one other thing you need to
know almost at once,' he added. 'That is——'

'How's Jolly?'

'Much better, but I wasn't thinking about Jolly. I was
thinking about the shops Golden Boy was supposed to have
owned under cover of a private company—it was the company
which first made us suspicious, and the fact that your cousin
was a shareholder.'

'*What?*'

'That's true. Jackson found it out.'

Rollison said abruptly: 'Well, what's to be done now?'

'George and Geraldine and Golden Boy won't be out of prison for at least ten years,' Grice answered. 'The shops could be sold, of course, but I thought you might consider taking them over, and gradually——'

'I know what to do with *those*!' cried Rollison in excitement. 'Two companies, with shares distributed among all those who suffered from the robberies. How does that sound?'

'I think it sounds very satisfying indeed,' said Grice.

It was deeply satisfying.

It helped to take some of the edge off the pain of the trials.

It gave Aunt Georgina plenty to think about, and Lady Hurst less cause for feeling ashamed.

It gave Jill Slater reward, too; being secretary of the two companies brought out all her better qualities and stopped her from brooding. She gave evidence first at the inquest, the verdict at which was 'justifiable homicide', then at the trial, where she did not spare herself or her dead husband, and so damned George and Geraldine not to ten but to fifteen years.

Bereft of a leader, freed from the malignant influence of Golden Boy, the youths who had served him drifted apart. Some fell for a life of idleness or petty crime, a few were already corrupted beyond redemption, but a fair proportion outgrew their vicious adolescence and became, in time, moderately satisfactory citizens.

The day after the trial was the day of the reopening of Rollison's flat, after the fire. It was resplendent with much that was new, nostalgic with much that was old, including everything on the Trophy Wall. Jolly, his old self again, opened the door in rapid succession to Old Glory, who looked magnificently Edwardian, to Grice and his wife, Jackson, Jill Slater, Bill Ebbutt, and, finally, Lady Georgina, who put a remarkably brave face on all that had happened.

'I know that out of consideration for my feelings you have added nothing to your wall,' she said, facing them with a courage that could, perhaps, have hidden the feelings to which she referred. 'But this was a very significant success, Richard, and you should have a memento.'

And with conscious ease and stoicism she placed upon the Trophy Wall a photograph of the twins.